LIVE OR DIE

For the next few frantic moments, fighting for his life, Fargo had
no wind to spare for waking up Rip. The attacker was strong and
swift, well versed in ground fighting, and he had his victim in a
literal death grip. Fargo held on to the brave's right wrist for dear
life, controlling the knife, but the determined warrior gouged at
Fargo's eyes with the fingers of his left hand.

They rolled in a confused tangle of limbs, the brave tenacious,
Fargo determined. He could smell the musty bear grease in the
Comanche's hair. Finally the Trailsman got his knees between
the two of them and tossed his assailant free just long enough to
jerk the Arkansas toothpick from his boot. This time, when the
brave leaped on him, he impaled himself on ten inches of cold,
lethally honed steel.

THE
TRAILSMAN
#339

RED RIVER
RECKONING

by

Jon Sharpe

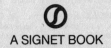

A SIGNET BOOK

SIGNET
Published by New American Library, a division of
Penguin Group (USA) Inc., 375 Hudson Street,
New York, New York 10014, USA
Penguin Group (Canada), 90 Eglinton Avenue East, Suite 700, Toronto,
Ontario M4P 2Y3, Canada (a division of Pearson Penguin Canada Inc.)
Penguin Books Ltd., 80 Strand, London WC2R 0RL, England
Penguin Ireland, 25 St. Stephen's Green, Dublin 2,
Ireland (a division of Penguin Books Ltd.)
Penguin Group (Australia), 250 Camberwell Road, Camberwell, Victoria 3124,
Australia (a division of Pearson Australia Group Pty. Ltd.)
Penguin Books India Pvt. Ltd., 11 Community Centre, Panchsheel Park,
New Delhi - 10 017, India
Penguin Group (NZ), 67 Apollo Drive, Rosedale, North Shore 0632,
New Zealand (a division of Pearson New Zealand Ltd.)
Penguin Books (South Africa) (Pty.) Ltd., 24 Sturdee Avenue,
Rosebank, Johannesburg 2196, South Africa

Penguin Books Ltd., Registered Offices:
80 Strand, London WC2R 0RL, England

First published by Signet, an imprint of New American Library,
a division of Penguin Group (USA) Inc.

First Printing, January 2010
10 9 8 7 6 5 4 3 2 1

The first chapter of this book previously appeared in *Texas Trackdown*, the three hundred
thirty-eighth volume in this series.

Copyright © Penguin Group (USA) Inc., 2010
All rights reserved

 REGISTERED TRADEMARK—MARCA REGISTRADA

Printed in the United States of America

The Trailsman

Beginnings . . . they bend the tree and they mark the man. Skye Fargo was born when he was eighteen. Terror was his midwife, vengeance his first cry. Killing spawned Skye Fargo, ruthless, cold-blooded murder. Out of the acrid smoke of gunpowder still hanging in the air, he rose, cried out a promise never forgotten.

The Trailsman they began to call him all across the West: searcher, scout, hunter, the man who could see where others only looked, his skills for hire but not his soul, the man who lived each day to the fullest, yet trailed each tomorrow. Skye Fargo, the Trailsman, the seeker who could take the wildness of a land and the wanting of a woman and make them his own.

Red River Valley, Indian Territory, 1860—where a murderous gang of river pirates holds a beautiful woman hostage, and Skye Fargo wages the fight of his life near the famous river that runs red—with blood.

1

A sudden hell-spawned yell split the silence of the lonely trail, raising the fine hairs on Skye Fargo's arms and tingling his scalp.

"Steady, old campaigner," he soothed his black-and-white pinto stallion as it stutter-stepped nervously backward. "It might kill us, but it won't eat us."

The crop-bearded, buckskin-clad man flicked the riding thong off the hammer of his single-action Colt and filled his hand. He sat his quivering horse in silent patience, shrewd, sun-crinkled lake blue eyes gazing ahead down a narrow trail.

On his left, a long and steep slope dense with brush and scrub oak led down to a timber-rich stretch of Red River, dividing the Indian Territory from Texas. On his right, the upward slope bristled with thick patches of hawthorn bushes, an ambusher's paradise.

A second time the hideous noise assaulted Fargo's ears, a demonic warbling from just ahead that again spooked the Ovaro. This time, however, Fargo recognized it.

"It's no devil," he assured his horse. "Just sounds like one. That's the Texas yell—but it's on the wrong side of the river."

Fargo hadn't heard the distinctive and unnerving Texas yell in years. The vengeful war cry had arisen after the massacre at the Alamo, and Texas Rangers had put it to good use fighting Kiowas and Comanches. But he never expected to hear it here in The Nations, as most men called the Indian Territory. Now more curious than nervous, Fargo tapped his heels, gigging the Ovaro forward.

Within moments he could hear a man who sounded drunk as the lords of creation belting out the lyrics to "Skip to My Lou." The hidden singer, his voice hoarse and rusty, next broke into "What Was Your Name in the States?"

Guiding himself by the awful singing, Fargo soon spotted a wayworn man and horse, both long in the tooth, lying sprawled on the steep slope below. Fargo couldn't see the man's face well under his slouched beaver hat, but his grizzled beard showed more salt than pepper, and a moccasin with a hard sole of buffalo hide covered his exposed right foot.

The horse, a ginger with a white mane, was dead from a broken neck. The man's left leg appeared to be trapped under the animal.

"Hush down, old-timer," Fargo called out. "You couldn't carry a tune in a bucket."

"That's Gospel, stranger, but my screechin' keeps off the buzzards."

"Looks like you could use a hand, old son. You stove up?"

"Nah. That leg's been busted before, and a busted bone knits stronger. But this damn horse has got me pinned."

Fargo leathered his Colt, then swung down and loosened the bridle. He dropped the bit before ground-tethering his stallion.

"I can smell forty-rod from here," he called down. "This ain't no trail to be riding drunk. Bad enough you killed your horse— that could be *your* neck that got snapped."

"No need to fling it in my teeth, boy. I ain't drunk. Would you believe this happened on account I ain't slept in ten whole days?"

"That's flat-out impossible," Fargo said.

"No, it ain't—I sleep at *night*."

The old man grinned broadly at his bad joke while Fargo shook his head. "Skeletons grin just like you are right now, you old fool."

"So what? Way I see it, skeletons ain't nothing but bones with the people scraped off."

"All right, cracker-barrel philosopher, I might's well just leave you where you are."

"Great jumpin' Judas! Don't leave me here, stranger—happens them Staked Plain Comanches find me, they'll slice off my eyelids under this blazin' sun."

"Simmer down, old bird dog; I'm just roweling you. I'll get you out. First I got a signal to send."

From where he stood, on the lip of the sandy trail, Fargo could see a supply-laden keelboat anchored under a white truce flag. He was serving as a contract scout for the freight-hauling firm of Russel, Majors & Waddell, which had recently added keel-boats to their line of conveyances. This one was hauling Arkansas goods west to the settlement at Wichita Falls, Texas.

Fargo removed a fragment of mirror from one of his saddle pockets and began flashing it toward the keelboat.

"The hell you doing?" the trapped man demanded.

"See that boat way down there? Whenever I have a line of sight, I signal the all-secure to them."

"All-secure, my sweet aunt."

"Spell that out," Fargo said, still flashing.

"Well, there's some stink brewing up in these parts, but I ain't caught a clear whiff of it yet."

"There's *always* stink brewing up in The Nations," Fargo reminded him. "That's been true ever since the government set it aside for the tribes. The place is an owlhoot paradise. By law, no Indian council can prosecute whites, and white man's law won't serve warrants on white criminals holed up here. Which leads a man to wonder what *you're* doing here."

"You an Indian lover? You didn't mention nothin' about red criminals."

"Quit dodging. What are you doing here?"

"Right now I'm laid out under a dead horse. You gonna help me or just stand there poking into my backtrail?"

Fargo waited for a return signal from the boat. The vessel was fifty-five feet long, with shallow sides that sloped inward. These formed a pen for the horses and mules grouped tightly behind a plank cabin amidships.

Fargo got the signal and put the mirror away. "No need to get all lathered up. Here I come."

Bracing his leg muscles against the steep angle, using sturdy brush for handholds, Fargo scrambled down. As he drew nearer, he saw the old roadster was an unequivocally homely man with coarse-grained skin, a careworn face, and a hawk nose.

"You ever hear of soap?" Fargo complained as he reached the trapped man's location. This close, he could see lice leaping from his clothing. "There's a stink around here, all right."

"I *am* a mite ripe," the man admitted. "I got no supplies. What's your name, son?"

Fargo knelt to get a closer look at the trapped leg. "Fargo. Skye Fargo."

The old man started. "Fargo? The same *hombre* some calls the Trailsman?"

"'Fraid so. I think I can lift this carcass up just enough for you to pull out from under it. It's only trapping your foot."

"Skye Fargo," the old man wondered aloud. "So *you're* the one can read sign on bare rock and track an ant across desert hardpan, huh?"

"Sure, and I can turn burro piss into wine, too. Never mind all that. . . . When I heave, jerk your foot out."

Fargo put his back to the horse's withers, took hold, and heaved, taut muscles straining like steel cables.

"Got 'er!" the old salt cried out jubilantly. He sat up, massaging his left foot. "You're strong as horseradish, Fargo."

"What's your name?" Fargo asked.

"Rip Miller. Ripley Alexander Miller the Third, to chew it fine."

Fargo snorted. "That's a thirty-five-cent mouthful. Rip is fine with me. Well, Rip, a word to the not-so-wise: You're out of your latitude here, Pop."

"Pop? Boy, a man is only as old as the women he feels."

Fargo fought back a grin, telling himself to remember that one. "Like I said, you're out of your latitude. Drunken saddle tramps don't stand a snowball's chance in The Nations."

"Saddle tramp? Hell's fire, you mouthy pup! Boy, I was scalpin' Kiowas while you was still on Ma's milk. Why, Rip Miller would wink into a rifle barrel. Saddle tramp, my sweet aunt. I prefer to call myself a bachelor of the saddle—same as you, from what I hear."

"If you're such a ripsnortin' *bravo*, the hell you doing slinking around the Indian Territory?"

"On account I got drunk and burned down a boardinghouse in Missouri, that's why. Strictly an accident, y'unnerstan'. Left Sedalia just ahead of a warrant."

"Like I figured—another damned owlhoot." In spite of himself, Fargo felt sorry for the old coot. He helped him to his feet. "How's that foot feel?"

"A mite ginger, but she'll come sassy. My cave ain't but a whoop and a holler from here, happens you don't mind riding double."

4

"You'll want this saddle," Fargo said.

"For a fact. Last thing I own. It's my rocking chair by day, my pillow by night."

Fargo undid the cinch and jerked the saddle free. He noticed the high, narrow horn and coiled around it the *cabristra*, a hair rope of the Texas style.

"Sorry about your horse," Fargo said, lugging the saddle over one shoulder and helping Rip up the slope with his free arm.

"Ah, that spavined son of a bitch never missed a chance to bite me on the ass. Won him in a poker game, and I'm glad to be shut of him."

They were just reaching the lip of the trail when Fargo's Ovaro gave his trouble whicker, a sound the Trailsman had learned over the years to respect. The two men gained the trail, and Fargo spotted them immediately: buzzards wheeling in the soft blue sky to the west, dark harbingers of death.

"Pile on the agony," he muttered.

"Could be a dead buff," Rip suggested. "Plenty around here."

"Could be," Fargo agreed, helping the old man up first.

But as Fargo turned the stirrup around and stepped into it, then pushed up and over, he couldn't help admitting it to himself: Trouble liked to dog the Trailsman like an afternoon shadow, and whatever waited for him up ahead, it was surely no dead buffalo.

"That stink you claimed is brewing up," Fargo said after they'd ridden for a few minutes, "you talking about Indian trouble or white-man trouble?"

"Both, likely. Been a lot more gunfire lately. All the tribes here in The Nations signed the Laramie Treaty back in 'fifty-one, but some just done it to get the presents. They never accepted the terms."

Fargo nodded. He'd fought renegades here before. "You saying some tribes have struck the war trail?"

"Nah, but some of the heap-big chiefs like Yellow Bear of the Staked Plain Comanches took their clans and jumped the rez. Now they like to swoop in here from the Texas Panhandle. They hit fast and hightail it back to the Llano."

Fargo's slitted gaze stayed in constant motion. Red River

was out of sight on their left now as the trail passed through sandy, hilly terrain interspersed with pines and granite cliffs. He could still see the buzzards, circling lower and lower.

"Folks cry you up big, Fargo," Rip said.

"Yeah, in the same newspapers they use to wipe their asses."

The smelly old drifter chuckled. "Both of us—dead broke and famous. Ain't it pitiful?"

"What makes you famous—the stench blowing off you?"

"If youth but knew. Sonny boy, you ever heard of Bob Coleman?"

"Who hasn't?" Fargo replied. "He was the first captain of the Texas Rangers."

"Ahuh, and I rode with him from 'thirty-five to 'thirty-nine. Fought Lipan Apaches, Kiowas, Comanches, and Mexers. Back then we didn't have Sam Colt's fancy revolvers like the one you got strapped on. Us Rangers was the best fighters and the best troublemakers."

"Best riders, too?" Fargo jibed. "Hell, Rip, that trail you fell off was twelve feet wide. Any fool could see the lip was loose sand."

"Pipe down, you jay! A jackrabbit spooked my horse."

"It's past mending now," Fargo relented. "I don't like all this screening timber. Stow the chinwag and keep that dragoon pistol of yours to hand."

They were riding nearer to whatever trouble lay ahead, and Fargo palmed the cylinder of his Colt to check the loads. Then he loosened his sixteen-shot, brass-framed Henry rifle in its saddle boot.

When the Ovaro began to sidestep, reluctant to proceed, Fargo felt a stirring of belly flies. His stallion was one to keep up the strut, and when he shied like this, Fargo knew trouble was on the spit.

"Steady, old warhorse," he soothed, patting the Ovaro's neck.

The rutted trail took a dogleg turn around a copse of pine trees. The sight that greeted both men, when they cleared the turn, made Fargo's gorge rise.

"God's trousers," Rip said in a voice just above a whisper. "Whoever done this ain't even fit to be called pond scum."

Fargo counted three dead men, one still slumped on the seat of a heavy freight wagon. All three sported numerous bullet

6

wounds, some astoundingly large, and had taken finishing shots in the forehead at close range—Fargo could see the powder burns on their skin.

"Shot to rag tatters," Rip said, anger tightening his voice. "Whoever done it even killed the horses."

Both men remained mounted, taking a careful look around.

"Like I was sayin'," Rip spoke up, "Comanches like to swoop into Red River country from the Llano. Goddamn featherheads. Neither Gospel nor gunpowder will ever tame them red devils."

"Red men didn't do this," Fargo gainsaid. "They'd use arrows and war hatchets for a job this easy. Besides, they never waste bullets on horses."

"I take your point. 'Sides, Comanches woulda lifted their dander and cut off their pizzles. These poor devils ain't been touched 'cept by bullets."

Fargo lit down and gave Rip a hand dismounting. Then the Trailsman began walking slow circles around the area, reading the signs.

"Four riders on shod horses," he concluded. "And at least one more driving a wagon. The wagon ruts are shallow coming in from the west, deeper heading back. They cleaned out whatever cargo was in this wagon."

"No damn wonder these boys couldn't defend theirselves," Rip said, picking up an old German fowling piece. "This old relic ain't much better'n a peashooter."

Fargo knelt to examine one of the corpses. "It didn't happen all that long ago. The blood's just now turning tacky."

Hearing this, Rip glanced nervously all around them. "Happens that's so, then ain't we paring the cheese mighty close to the rind? Fargo, I fair got the fidgets. Them killers coulda left a rear guard, and he could be droppin' a bead on *us* right now. Let's rustle."

Fargo nodded, standing back up. "They might've played it that way to make sure they get away with the freight— Say, what's that?"

A sheet of paper protruding from a dead man's pocket had caught Fargo's eye. He pulled it out and unfolded it. It was an official right-of-transit letter bearing the Bureau of Indian Affairs seal.

"That's what I figured," he told Rip. "These were civilian contract freighters. Every spring they bring in the issue of annuities to the rez Indians. Blankets, coffee, flour, sugar, bacon and such. We best—"

A bullet tore through the letter in Fargo's hand and thwacked into the freight wagon less than a heartbeat before the crack of a high-power rifle reached both men. The slug was so big it tore out a fist-sized chunk of the wood.

"Hell's a-poppin'!" Rip shouted, scrambling under the wagon as another bullet snapped past Fargo's head so close he felt a line of heat.

2

Fargo couldn't leave his Ovaro exposed. The untethered stallion was bullet trained and hadn't fled when the shooting began. With more slugs fanning him, Fargo tugged his Henry from its boot, then smacked the black-and-white pinto on its glossy rump, sending it into the nearby pine trees.

"Fargo, you fool, cover down!" Rip shouted from under the wagon. "That bastard's got some good artillery!"

The Trailsman needed no invitation. He dropped straight to the ground and rolled under the wagon, bullet plumes chasing him all the way.

"You spotted his position?" Fargo demanded as he jacked a round into the Henry's chamber.

"Hell no! Black powder smokes like a freight engine, but the trees are holding it down. He's dug in like a tick on a hound."

More dirt plumes kicked up as the shooter tried to range his shots under the wagon. Usually, when he couldn't spot powder smoke, Fargo tried to use bullet angle to trace the shots back to the gun. But the hilly terrain and dense cover made that impossible.

"Christ, he's finding his range," Rip warned when a slug kicked dirt in his face.

Fargo had to settle for his fallback strategy: he picked a probable sector of fire and relied on the Henry's magazine capacity to pepper the area with lead. Left elbow dug in behind a wagon wheel, he repeatedly levered and fired, ejector port clicking like a mantel clock as hot shell casings spewed out around the two men.

He fired all sixteen loads in less than thirty seconds, silencing the shooter. Moments later, the rataplan of shod hooves sounded behind the nearby line of hills. Both men remained under the wagon.

"Goin' after the son of a buck?" Rip demanded.

Fargo checked the time by the slant of the sun. Then he whistled in the Ovaro.

"Not now," he replied. "It's nigh onto dark, and this stretch of Red River country is likely his home range. Besides, we can't catch him riding double, and we need to get you to your cave."

"Great jumpin' Judas, Fargo, what kind of weapon was that dry-gulcher firing? I know there's repeatin' rifles now like the Volcanic and your Henry, but *that* one what almost done for us is calibrated like a Sharps buff gun."

Fargo shook his head as the two men scooted cautiously out from under the wagon. "The Spencer carbine is .56 caliber, but this weapon holds way more shells. I'm thinking it's a gun-shop special: custom-made for a cold-blooded killer."

He looked at the bodies, his face grim and determined. "I'm not a practicing Christian, Rip, but they deserve burying. I've got a U.S. Army entrenching tool lashed to my saddle."

"Sure, we'll bury 'em. Will that be the end of it, Fargo?"

Fargo started to untie the small shovel. "I'm not the law, and it's not my job to solve every murder I stumble across. Besides, I'm under contract to do a job. But when that skunk-bitten coyote tried to kill *me*, it suddenly got personal. There's at least five killers in the mix, and since there's no law in The Nations, I intend to point their toes toward the sky."

A spark of admiration glinted in Rip's rheumy old eyes. "By God, so it's true what they say about the Trailsman. *He's* the law when there's no other."

"Oh, you admire that, do you?" Fargo grinned wickedly. "I'm glad to hear it because I'm going to need a 'deputy.' And I can't think of a better man to ride the river with than a Texas Ranger—even one as old as Methuselah."

Rip puffed his chest out like a strutting rooster. "You'll see—I'll do to take along. But what about that keelboat?"

"There's no tight schedule, and I'm on friendly terms with the captain. We'll go explain this deal and borrow you a horse. But I'm honor bound to warn you, old-timer—if all five of those men are armed like the one who almost killed us, this will be a rough piece of work. The kind they advertise under 'Orphans Preferred.' "

"That's the way of it, Etienne," Fargo told the leader of the twelve voyageurs, the New Orleans Creoles who manned the keelboat. "I know you don't like delays, but I think a few days might be enough to put the quietus on this murdering gang."

Etienne, wiry and tough, was tanned dark as a Creek Indian. He had listened carefully to Fargo's account of the day's events.

"As for me, Monsieur Fargo," he said in heavily accented English, "I am willing to take the risk of camping here. But *these . . ."*

He nodded toward a big campfire nearby on the riverbank. The Creoles were enjoying their nightly rum ration in the gathering darkness, gambling and singing lewd songs in French.

"They were hired to man the poles and tow ropes when the wind is against us. They know this is Indian country, and they want only to get through it as quickly as possible. A few days camp here? *Ciel!* They might cut my throat."

"They like you better than that," Fargo said. "And Mr. Majors supplied each man with a repeating rifle and a bandolier of ammo. Most of the trouble-seeking Indians along Red River are just renegade bands without firearms. Besides, they're hit-and-run fighters—like to catch just a few of their enemy out in the open. They won't attack a forted-up position like this camp."

"'Sides that," Rip chimed in, "it's likely these white killers are more dangersome than Injins."

Again Etienne nodded. "I agree. But my men and I, we are from the city, and knives are the only weapons we know. Still . . . if you think it is best to camp here a few days, Monsieur Fargo, I trust your judgment. At least two keelboats have disappeared on this river recently."

"Majors gave you extra rum," Fargo reminded him as Etienne rose from the fire. "Try to sweeten the deal with that."

"Hell, Fargo, you think they *are* safe here?" Rip asked when the ramrod was out of hearing range.

"New Orleans is a rough place, and the fact these Creoles are still alive proves they're tough. I've seen them on the scrap, and they're no boys to fool with. This bunch ain't cowards—it's just, they hear so many tales about 'wild Indians,' and most have never seen a Plains warrior. Ask them, they'll swear a typical brave is twelve-feet tall and eats white men."

A damp chill had set in, and Fargo paused to stir up the fire.

"Besides that," he added, "those killers up in the bluffs are after supplies. This boat is hauling a hell of a lot more than a freight wagon can carry. For now, I'd rather have these fellows in numbers on the bank than out there on the river, exposed to rifle fire."

The two men fell silent, listening as Etienne spoke to the men in French. Several of them sent surly glances toward the two white men. A few more spoke up in spirited protest. Fargo knew very little French, but he recognized the word *peaux-rouges* repeated often: redskins.

"Them frogs is hot-tempered," Rip said. "Looks like you started a mutiny, Fargo."

A moment later, however, Etienne leaped aboard the anchored boat. He returned with four bottles of rum. A cheer went up from the crew.

"Mutiny over," Fargo announced. "Now let's cut you out a horse."

A broad, strong plank led from the grassy bank to the low deck of the boat. Fargo took Rip into the slope-sided pen.

"There's six horses," he told the old-timer, "all wild mustangs broke to leather. You can have your pick."

The voyageurs' big fire threw plenty of light onto the boat. Rip studied each horse, mostly concentrating on the eyes.

"I favor thissen," he finally announced, settling on a dapple-gray with a shaggy mane. "That broom-tail needs to be cut, but looks to me like this scrub has got what the dons call *brio escondido*—hidden vigor."

Fargo nodded approval. "You know horseflesh, all right. That's my favorite, too. Only fourteen hands, but those short, stout legs are hard to injure. I've watched these Indian ponies outrun grain-fed, seventeen-hand Cavalry sorrels."

An owl hoot sounded as the two men led the mustang off the boat.

"That weren't no owl," Rip said.

"Some tribe or other is watching the camp," Fargo agreed. "Why not? This is their land, and they always watch trespassers. Especially along the Texas border."

Rip put the dapple-gray on a long tether close to Fargo's Ovaro. "The featherheads are damn fools," he scoffed as they returned to the fire. "They hate bein' here in The Nations, am I right?"

"Right as rain."

"Well, by God, they wouldn't *be* here if they wasn't always warrin' amongst theirselves. Coulda banded the tribes together and killed the paleface off long before the Oregon Trail was blazed. Hell, the Cherokees are so damn smart they had their own newspapers, yet they took to killin' one another. Now they'll take the white man's land leavin's and eat government pork. Damn fools."

Fargo shook his head, dishing up a plate of rabbit stew and pan bread. "There's some truth in all that, Rip. They're almost whipped, all right, and they'll all soon be dead, in prison, or answering roll calls on a rez. But they're not fools—just notional. They let their hearts rule their heads."

"Ahuh, mebbe you're right, Fargo. They say you got big medicine with some of the tribes. Me, I don't hate Injins. But after tanglin' with Comanch and Kiowa at Blanco Canyon, I ain't no Injin lover, neither. Them two tribes is death to the devil, and there's a bunch down in east Texas are damn cannibals."

Rip interrupted himself to fart loudly, sending Fargo quickly upwind of him. "Kiss for ya, Trailsman. But like I was sayin', the red men is savages—everybody knows that. Us whites is mostly Christians, goddamn it. But what we seen today, Fargo, makes me ireful. And some dry-gulching bastard trying to send *us* under, too."

Fargo nodded, his nut brown face grim as death in the dancing firelight. "It won't stand, Rip. I put my cast-iron guarantee on that."

After supper, Fargo and Rip moved their mounts in closer to the camp, leaving the tethers long enough so the horses could drink from the river and graze the lush grass. Then Fargo sat in the firelight to run a bore patch through his rifle and place a drop of gun oil on the works.

"You seen them storm clouds makin' up earlier?" Rip fretted.

Fargo nodded. "There's a ring around the moon, too. Looks like we got a gully washer coming."

"Happens that's so, there goes the killers' trail."

"We might not need it," Fargo speculated. "They have to be hauling those goods somewhere. It's been a while since I rode Red River country—any settlements in these parts?"

"I been slingin' hash in Sedalia these past three years. But, on the Texas side of the river, there ain't nothin' 'tween Texarkana and Wichita Falls. On this side, there ain't nothin' legal. But saloon gossip claims there's trading post settlements by them as bribed the blue-bellies. I ain't seen none, though. You don't see much when you're hid out in a cave."

Full dark had settled over them, and buttery moonlight reflected off the river. The current made a pleasant, steady, chuckling noise. Fargo laid his rifle, six-shooter, and Arkansas toothpick handy. Then he pulled a hog-bristle toothbrush from a saddle pocket and began working his teeth with it while he conned over the day's events.

Rip watched him, perplexed. "Why would a man wash his teeth?"

"So he can eat more than mush, that's why."

"Happens that remark's aimed at me, mebbe I got no jaw teeth left, but I'm your boy when the war whoop sounds. My calves ain't gone to grass just yet."

"You'll get the chance to prove it," Fargo promised him. "Don't forget, we're up against at least one repeating rifle that can knock down a barn with one shot."

Rip rolled up in a new blanket Etienne had given him, resting his head on his saddle. "I know why you fuss over them choppers, Fargo. I 'magine a stallion like you likes to chase after the dolly birds, uh?"

Fargo removed the brush and frowned at his companion. "What else would I chase after . . . sheep?"

"Honest, constable—I was only helping that sheep over the fence."

Rip laughed himself into a hacking cough while Fargo shook his head. "You're soft-brained, old man."

Fargo laid his yellow slicker to hand in case of rain and rolled up in his blanket, comfortable and content. But the sad, soft whisper in the pines made even a bunch quitter like him feel lonesome—until the owl hoots that weren't *really* owl hoots reminded him he had company.

3

Fargo whistled in the Ovaro and wiped the morning dew off the pinto's back, tossing on blanket, pad, and saddle. While Fargo worked, the stallion pushed his nose into Fargo's sleeve, greeting him.

"Weren't much rain last night," Rip observed as he tacked his Indian scrub nearby.

"Not on us," Fargo called back. "But I heard it coming down in sheets just west of us, and that's where we're headed."

Fargo slid the bridle over his stallion's ears and buckled the throat latch. Then he tied a big sack of parched corn to the saddle horn. It was one of Fargo's favorite foods, when hunting wasn't practical, because both horse and rider could eat it.

The two men left the riverbank camp before the mist had burned off, gnawing on heels of cold pone for breakfast as they rode.

"Got any eating 'baccy?" Rip demanded.

"Just some Mexican shag for smoking."

Rip looked disgusted. "Ain't nobody clings to the old ways."

"Nothing suits your fancy, Queen Victoria, does it?"

"Hell, I apologize, Fargo. Yestiddy you kept me from becomin' buzzard bait. I appreciate the hell right out of that."

Fargo grinned. "You might not be so grateful by the time this deal is over. I got a God fear we're up against it, Rip."

"Won't matter much if *I* get my wick snuffed—my woman-topping days is long over. But think of all the slap 'n' tickle *you* stand to lose."

"Hell," Fargo said, "when you put it that way . . ."

Both men laughed, the sound quickly swallowed up by the river just to their left. The Ovaro, still shaking out the night kinks, wanted to bust loose. So Fargo spurred his mount from trot, to pace, to lope, finally to a gallop. But the stallion still fought the reins, wanting his head, so Fargo let him out to a full run, barely catching his hat in time when it almost flew off.

Soon, however, the ground grew softer from last night's downpour, and Fargo reined back to a trot.

"Katy Christ!" Rip swore when he finally caught up. "I thought you two was gonna ride into the middle of next week!"

"We best bear north up into the bluffs," Fargo said. "See if we can pick up any sign of those killers."

But the condition of the ground—in places, sloppy as gumbo—did not augur well. When they reached the spot of the ambush and the abandoned wagon, Fargo dismounted and studied the ground.

"Mostly washed out," he reported. "We know they had to follow the trail at first, but these bluffs are hard going for a conveyance. Eventually they must've gone back down to the river flat. Problem is, where?"

They rode the long bluff for the better part of an hour. Fargo occasionally spotted a faint rut that hadn't washed out. He always assumed there were bushwhackers up in the rim rock, and his eyes constantly scanned above.

The late-spring day heated up, ragged parcels of cottony cloud drifting across a deep blue dome of sky. Fargo watched a yellow-gray coyote slink off through a dry wash, grinning at some sly secret.

"Damn it, Fargo," Rip spoke up. "There's a hoodoo on me or somethin'."

"Spell that out plain."

"I can't put words to it, but somethin' just don't feel right. We're about to get the hurt dance did on us."

"I'm sorry to hear you say that," Fargo admitted. "Back of my neck's been tingling almost since we rode out, and every time it does that, I ride into a shit storm."

"So we're both hitchin' to the same rail? That means we best keep our powder dry and our peckers hard."

Fargo nodded. "You make sense when you're sober."

"As to that . . ." Rip pulled a bottle of rum from a saddle pocket. "Etienne give it to me. Happens I'm about to die, might's well have me a taste."

"Gradual on that," Fargo warned when Rip took his second

17

and third swallows. "Look what happened last time you got shellacked."

"Save your breath to cool your porridge! Coffin varnish?" Rip added, proffering the bottle.

"Don't care if I do." Fargo knocked back a slug, feeling the rum burn a hot beeline to his stomach. "Let's head down to the river, see if we can pick up any sign."

Fargo scoured the flat terrain to no avail. If riders and a wagon had passed this way, last night's violent storm had covered their tracks.

"There's a break in the bluffs," he said, pointing north. "Let's ride through and see if we cross any tracks."

Now and then, as they trotted their mounts north, the terrain closed in, numerous tangled coverts affording ambush spots. From years of scouting, Fargo had learned to send his hearing out beyond the near distances. Something he detected in the wind made him dismount and place three fingertips lightly on the ground.

"Feels like riders coming this way fast," he said. "And judging from the feel, their horses ain't shod."

"Yep, there's a hoodoo on us," Rip said in a grim tone. "Too many trees out ahead of us, but I don't see no dust puffs."

"Ground's still too wet," Fargo reminded him.

He cast his eye all around them and spotted a slight, wooded rise. Fargo hit leather again, veered off toward the rise, then scaled the tallest tree.

"Well, I'm a Dutchman!" he called down to Rip. "It's Indians, all right."

"By the twin balls of Christ! Comanches?"

"I can't tell yet—they're too far out. But they must've had a scout out, old son, because they're riding a plumb line straight toward us. And judging from that war formation, they ain't too glad to see us."

Fargo started down the tree twice as fast as he'd gone up.

"How many?" Rip demanded.

"Maybe a dozen, fifteen. Renegades, I'd wager," Fargo replied. "Could be attacking from Antelope Hills—that's the most notorious haven in the Indian Territory."

"And us trapped between the sap and the bark," Rip said, glancing wide-eyed all around them. They were still only about halfway through the saddle between bluffs, making escape to east or west difficult because of steep, open slopes. Riding north would take them right at the attackers—the only open route was south back to the river.

Fargo realized all this too. "We'll dust our hocks back toward Red River. The tribes living in peace are denied horses and guns by the treaty. Which means this bunch are prob'ly raiders."

"That likely spells Kiowas or Comanches—or both," Rip said as Fargo swung up into leather and wheeled the Ovaro. "Our tits are in the wringer, boy. Both them tribes is poison mean."

"Gee up!" Fargo snapped at the Ovaro, thumping his flanks with both heels.

Fargo put his chin in the mane, riding hell-bent for election. He quickly realized, however, that he'd have to cut back the pace. Unlike the Ovaro, Rip's mustang had been penned up on the river for weeks and was not yet up to full fettle.

Unfortunately for the fleeing men, it was the Plains Indian custom to slit their horses' nostrils for extra wind. Before long, Fargo glanced over his shoulder and spotted red-streamered war lances. Rip had seen them too.

"God kiss me!" he shouted above the rapid drumbeat of hooves. "It's Comanches, right enough! And the way their faces is greased, they mean to paint the landscape red with *our* blood. At the rate they're gainin', we'll never make the river."

"Swallow your gizzard," Fargo ordered sharply. "We'll make it. If you were truly a Texas Ranger, then you know how to make a horse run faster."

Rip remembered the old days immediately and stretched forward across the pommel, seizing the mustang's left ear in his mouth and clamping down hard. In a burst of anger, the Indian scrub surged from a hard gallop to a flat-out run.

Nonetheless, the Comanches had grown dangerously close. Fargo knew their fox-skin quivers were stuffed with deadly quartz-tipped arrows—arrows their bows, strung with tough buffalo sinew, could hurl up to four hundred yards. And a Comanche could launch up to fifteen a minute with his pony at a dead run.

The first arrows fwipped past them now, making the Ovaro and the mustang run even faster. By the time they reached the

north bank of the river, both mounts were lathered and blowing foam.

"You cross first," Fargo ordered his trail partner. "Soon's you ford, wrestle your horse down for a breastwork."

Like most western rivers, the Red always dried up to a trickle stream by late summer. Right now, however, it was full of new snowmelt and rushing with a fast current. Both men charged in until their horses were swimming, then slid backward to grab their tails, letting the mounts pull them across.

"Hell!" Rip shouted above the roar of the river and the din of closing Indians. "Let's just grab leather and hightail it deeper into Texas!"

"Texas never stopped them before. Our best chance is the river."

Fargo had no time to explain it now, but he definitely had a strategy—and it centered around his observation that very few Indians would risk dying in water. Even the fiercest brave feared an "unclean" death, and drowning, like hanging, was spiritually unclean. Since many tribes believed the last moment of their lives was the moment they lived eternally in the afterlife, no man wanted to risk drowning forever.

The two men struggled onto the opposite bank, and Fargo quickly led them back about twenty yards from the water. The Ovaro, trained in this trick, lay down flat the moment Fargo encircled his neck and tugged. Rip's mustang, however, fought his new rider.

Fargo grabbed an old feed sack, used for rubbing down the Ovaro, from a saddle pocket and pulled it over the mustang's head. The dapple-gray lay down immediately.

"Fargo, your trail craft is all it's cracked up to be," Rip praised as he took up a position behind his horse. "Now you'll see how good I can still aim this old dragoon pistol."

"Nix on that," Fargo said. "Don't shoot to kill the warriors. Just drop a couple of their horses. We don't want a blood vendetta with Comanches."

"But—"

"Stick your 'buts' back in your pocket, old-timer. These ain't your ranger days. We're just little fish to these renegades, and we're gonna keep it that way. If they get blood in their eyes, you and me are gone beavers."

Fargo dashed back to his supine stallion, arrows blurring the air around his head. By now the braves were so close he could easily make out the dyed porcupine quills trimming their buckskin leg bands. The commotion of their war shrieks made the Ovaro tremble.

But Fargo's hunch panned out—none of the braves seemed eager to enter the river while guns were trained on them, thus risking unclean death. However, with arrows ripping into the grass all around the horses, the battle was in full pitch, and Fargo knew it wouldn't be long before one or both mounts were hit.

"Rip!" he shouted. "That dragoon pistol sounds and smokes like a cannon—it'll impress them. Drop a horse."

"*Now* you're whistlin', Fargo!"

The Colt dragoon exploded, and a claybank mustang dropped like a stone, almost trapping its rider's legs. Another brave took the rider up behind him. Fargo levered and fired the Henry several times, trimming warbonnets and puncturing buffalo-hide shields.

The main body moved back out of easy range, but refused to retreat. One of the braves, waving a coup stick covered with white eagle tail feathers, separated from the rest and galloped upstream.

"Christ!" Rip fretted. "They're going to ford at another spot and rush us! We best start killing them now."

"Hold off," Fargo ordered. "That brave is going to count coup on one of us to show he's the big he-bear. They have to save face for the lost horse. Don't shoot him, or this won't end until we're dead as last Christmas."

"Lord Almighty with a wooden leg, Fargo! You're gonna trust a Comanche? That's a coup stick in one hand, sure. But the other's holdin' a war hatchet."

"Never mind 'trust,' you chucklehead. It's just sound battle tactics. If we kill that brave, the rest will hound us into hell. Stay frosty, old son."

The brave forded and raced down the bank toward their position, his mustang's hooves flinging divots of dirt and grass.

Fargo pointed his rifle, but didn't aim it. Rip looked white as new linen.

"Yiii-eee-*yah*!"

The Comanche leaped his pony over Rip's position and bore relentlessly down on Fargo. The flat coup stick caught the Trailsman squarely across the shoulder blades, stinging like rock salt.

The brave charged into the river, still shrieking, as a triumphant cry rose from the rest. A minute later, the band retreated to the north.

"I'll be hog-tied and earmarked," Rip said, his voice still high and cracked from fright. "Fargo, you are some pumpkins. A Texas Ranger knows how to kill redskins, but you know how to *think* like 'em. You just saved our bacon."

"Save your hoorays," Fargo warned, letting the Ovaro stand up. "Like we were saying last night, Indians are notional. This bunch prob'ly wants bigger game than us, but if they don't find it, we'll be their favorite boys. Anyhow, we got other fish to fry, and we're burning daylight."

4

Their horses had been run hard and were matted with sweat. So after fording back to the north bank and tethering them in the lush river grass to graze and drink, both men stripped their mounts down to the neck leather. They examined them for saddle galls before checking each hoof for cracks or stone bruises.

Fargo fished a hoof pick from his possibles bag and removed a few small stones from the Ovaro's hooves.

"Fargo," Rip said as they spread the sweat-soaked saddle blankets out on hot rocks to dry, "what's the roughest set-to you ever had?"

"I don't think about all the scrapes. Hell, when I look at it logically, I'm already dead."

Rip chuckled. "Thissen today had me shittin' strawberries, and you just as cool as winter snowpack. Been twenty years since I rode with Captain Coleman, and I'm a mite rusted up in the hinges."

"You did all right," Fargo assured him, eyes scanning in all directions.

"You're a leader, not a boss, that's how's come. Fargo, you can lead a Texan, but you can't boss him. That's on account the U.S. let Texas into the Union but they won't defend her. Makes us Lone Star boys scrappy."

Forgo nodded. The no-surrender doctrine he himself lived by had evolved out of the early, bloody turmoil of the Republic of Texas days. And he was beginning to suspect another fight to the death awaited them here in The Nations—if not with Comanches, then with cold-blooded white killers who knew no law restrained them.

While the blankets dried, they ate a few handfuls of parched corn.

"We lookin' for that trail again?" Rip asked.

Fargo shook his head. "It's taking too much time, and I want to make sure those renegades aren't hanging around. You said last night there's talk of illegal settlements north of the Red."

"Ahuh. Talk. Ain't never seen one, but mostly I stayed holed up in a cave since I come here."

"If you study on it," Fargo said, "whoever heisted those annuities has to have some place to sell them, and it sure's hell won't be to Indians—the tribes get them for free."

"So it's likely a settlement, huh? At least a trading post?"

Fargo nodded. "A few trading posts are legal. But just think how it would sweeten the profits if the owners didn't have to lay out cash for stock?"

Rip whistled. "At these prices on the frontier? Hell, I know of blankets goin' for twenty dollars."

"The way you say, Texas. But the last trading post I saw, behind us, was just outside of Arkansas. So, assuming the next one would be built on a waterway, our best bet is to keep pushing west along the river."

"That shines," Rip agreed. "Damn it, Fargo, it's been rough sledding down in south Texas since I was a pup on the rug. But they was a time when a man could move through these northern diggin's and not get shot to doll stuffin's. The West is goin' to hell in a hay wagon, by God."

Fargo knew that better than any man alive. Newspapers, back east in the Land of Steady Habits, called the Missouri River "the end of civilization." Beyond it there were no railroads, no telegraphs, and barely enough white men to justify a scant U.S. Army presence. Fargo wished things would stay that way, but "progress" was already arriving, and fences, taxes, and rapid destruction of the pristine land would be right on its heels.

"Blankets're dry," he said, "and the horses have cooled off. C'mon, old ranger, let's saddle up."

By late afternoon the sun burned high in the sky as if pegged there. The two men had followed the grassy bank of the Red River at an easy trot, eyes in constant motion.

"God's galoshes!" Rip swore, slapping at his neck. "This latest hatch of flies are cannibals."

Mosquitoes had plagued them all night in camp, now it was

flies all day. Both horses snuffled in irritation, shaking their manes and tails to ward them off.

Fargo rarely let such irritants distract him. The terrain on their right flank was mostly low hills with scattered pine growth and some steep razorbacks well to the north of the river. In places near the Red, the grass grew high as the knuckles of a full-grown buffalo. Fargo studied all of it with steady vigilance, knowing danger could come from any quarter.

"I never top a woman in a strawberry patch, Fargo," Rip spoke up. "Know why?"

Rip was the type who would wait forever, so Fargo said, "Why?"

"Because she'll have her ass in a jam!"

Fargo snorted while Rip practically laughed himself out of the saddle. "Get it? Strawberry—"

"I get it, I get it. Leave that bottle alone," Fargo snapped when Rip reached for a saddle pocket. "Save it for when we make camp. This ain't no Sunday stroll."

"Now you're bossin', not leadin'."

"Tough shit. You don't like it, go work for those Comanches."

Rip grinned. "I can stomach a boss."

By now the day's heat was like a furnace blast. Fargo whipped the dust from his hat, then sleeved sweat off his forehead. With his eyes cleared, he spotted a curl of black smoke snaking into the sky past the next bend in the river.

"Could be trouble ahead, Rip," he cautioned. "Make sure all your cylinders are capped and your powder loads haven't clumped. But *don't* go starting any shooting forays. We're looking for evidence right now, not targets."

Nonetheless, Fargo remembered that high-power repeating rifle from yesterday and knocked the rawhide thong off the hammer of his Colt.

"By the Lord Harry," Rip muttered when they came out of the next bend. "Is it Sodom or Gomorrah?"

The abysmal sight awaiting their eyes was not really a town, or even a settlement—just a warren of canvas dens, at its muddy hub, with a winding maze of wagon ruts snaking through them. A handful of wretched mud hovels had sprung up like toadstools on the periphery. Empty bottles, rusted cans, and various bones—animal and human—dotted the area.

"No school or churches," Fargo edified his companion, tone dripping sarcasm.

But what held both men's attention was a large walled compound at the far end of this pimple on nowhere's ass. The walls of the compound were loop-holed for rifles. A gate in the east wall stood open, and both men could clearly see it contained a huge, split-log cabin, an open-front shed for horses, and near the gate, a smithy—source of all the smoke.

"We found our trading post," Rip announced.

"*A* trading post," Fargo corrected him. "We got no evidence this place is linked to the jaspers who killed those teamsters and fired on us."

"Captain Coleman's motto was, 'Kill 'em all and let God sort 'em out.'"

"Bully for him. *My* motto is, 'Never stack your conclusions higher than your evidence.' C'mon, let's ride in, and keep your eyes to all sides, Rip. I've seen holes like this, down in Mexico, where they shoot a man for his boots."

They let their nervous horses walk through the rutted swale that passed for a street. The "fanciest" dwelling, outside the walled compound and its large cabin, was a sod house with a dwarf cliff as a back wall. Two groups of horses, bridles down, marked a pair of canvas saloons. Crudely painted boards over the doorways announced one as the BUCKET OF BLOOD, the other the SAWDUST CORNER.

"Bet you a plugged peso both them watering holes double as undertaker's parlors," Rip said. "No need to lug the corpses anywhere."

"Judging from the human bones scattered everywhere, they don't bother with such formalities in these parts."

Fargo felt shadowy eyes watching them from the saloons, but the shabby settlement was hardly a beehive of activity, and there was no sign of the usual gawkers. They rode through the open gate of the trading post and spotted a swarthy, heavyset man with hairy hands working a bellows in the smithy.

"Howdy," Fargo called out from the saddle. "Any chance you could file down a couple horseshoes for me?"

In fact Fargo carried his own horseshoe file and hammer in a saddle pocket, but he needed information and didn't relish the idea of looking for it in those canvas saloons.

26

"Justin Halfpenny, at your service, gents," the blacksmith replied. "That's easy work, stranger. Just tell me which ones and leave your horse—fine-looking beast. Uncut stallion, I see."

Fargo liked this fellow's manner, but he had no intention of leaving the Ovaro out of his sight in this tented berg. The pinto was a magnet for horse thieves.

"Actually," he said, "they're my spares. I'll just leave them while I'm in the trading post."

At mention of the trading post, Halfpenny's bearded face was transformed into a mask of conflicting feelings. Glancing carefully around, he lowered his voice.

"I see you two are strangers. Watch out for them Winslowe brothers, hear? There's four of them, all so poison mean they'd shoot a man for snoring. Don't put your back to any of them."

"They own the trading post?" Fargo pressed.

"Stone does. He's the oldest. The others do his bidding."

Fargo and Rip exchanged a quick glance.

"Don't sound like you've got much use for them," Fargo said.

"Why should I? Ask them, they own every raccoon that craps on their back forty. They figure there ain't room in the puddle but for one big frog, and that frog is them."

"Is Stone's place licensed by the army?" Fargo asked.

"Stranger, there's plenty more things I wish I could say, but I dursn't. A grave is a cold and lonely place."

Fargo nodded. "If that's the way of it, don't fret none. You said nothing to us."

"Well, I figured you didn't need no shoes filed, if you take my drift? I like the cut of you, mister—you look like exactly the kind of man we need hereabouts. Only, don't make *no* mistakes with them four. Satan himself calls them sir."

Fargo touched his hat and the two men rode across a packed-dirt yard.

"For a man big enough to fight cougars with a shoe," Rip remarked, "that hombre is scared spitless."

Fargo nodded. "'Pears that way."

"Look." Rip pointed down. "Deep wagon ruts."

"Quit pointing, you damn fool," Fargo muttered. "I see 'em. It's a trading post, remember? You think they *miracle* their stock onto the shelves?"

"No, but they didn't squat next to a river just so's they'd have a place to piss. Likely, their goods come by water."

"Even so, what comes in must go out. Customers could have made those tracks. Never mind wagon ruts—before I pull down on a man, I need solid proof."

They reached a corner of the big split-log cabin and swung down, wrapping their reins around the tie rail and dropping the bridles.

"Listen, old-timer," Fargo said in a voice just above a whisper as he loosened his saddle cinch a notch, "*we* don't make the battle plan. Our enemy does. Keep mum inside and play along with whatever I say. But if you see me clear leather, jerk back that smoke wagon of yours and set to work."

Fargo lifted the rawhide thong that served as a latchstring and stepped through the doorway into the hot, smoky, sweat-stinking dimness within. The interior of the log-cabin trading post was cram-jammed with all manner of supplies: blankets, clothing for both sexes, wagon canvas, sacks of sugar, flour and meal, shoes and boots, saddles, bridles, harnesses. Rifles and handguns hung from nails on the wall, and wooden bins were stuffed with lead balls sorted by caliber. Shelves held flasks of black powder and cartons of the new factory-pressed cartridges.

Fargo had traded at dozens of frontier posts. Never, however, had he seen one this well stocked. And where were the customers?

However, his study of the inventory was cut short by a pleasant sight that made Fargo suddenly forget to breathe.

"Moses on the mountain!" Rip whispered from just behind him, and Fargo realized the old ranger had spotted her too.

Fargo considered himself a knowledgeable judge of female flesh, and the specimen he spotted now, waving a feather fly swisher around to shoo away the buzzing pests, took the blue ribbon. He took in curled hair the color of new wheat, flawless skin like a fine lotion, delicately carved cheeks that glowed like Roman Beauties—and a rose taffeta dress that showed more well-placed curves than a man could brake for.

The ominous click of a hammer being thumb-cocked broke Fargo's spell.

"Tomcattin' don't go around here, mister. Savvy that? That's my brother's wife you're undressing with your eyes."

Fargo had been so entranced by the woman that he hadn't even noticed the two men inside the trading post. The one behind the counter towered over six feet and had a rock-solid jaw, a thin mustache, and hard, aggressive eyes that bored through him like lance points.

But it was the man lounging against a side wall, watching him from angry eyes like molten metal, who held a cocked Remington trained on Fargo.

"Brother, you have my motives all wrong," Fargo assured him meekly. "Yes, I did stare at this wondrous creature. She is an excellent example of God's marvelous handiwork—an example rarely seen on the frontier. But my thoughts were not lustful."

The man gave a harsh bark of laughter. "I ain't your fuckin' 'brother.' The hell you mean, 'God's handiwork'?"

"I am a humble servant of the Lord, friend."

The man's skeptical gaze swept Fargo's length. "S'at so? You sure's hell don't *look* like no preacher."

"You'll find all types toiling in God's vineyards, my friend."

"In a pig's ass. Like I said, you sure's hell don't look like the type who spends his evenings reading psalms. And that old flea-bag siding you didn't get that ugly red nose from sippin' sarsaparilla."

Rip swore under his breath. Out loud he said, "Listen, you—"

"Father, turn the other cheek," Fargo cut him off, hoping the others didn't notice when Rip's eyes bulged out in astonishment at being called "Father." Fargo trusted no man who oiled his holster and wore his gun below his hip as this one did—the sure sign of a professional killer.

"No man with sap in him takes to Bible-thumpin'," the bully snarled. "You figure bein' a holy man will spare you from a beatin'?"

Fargo knew his preacher scheme was dodgy. But he also suspected these Winslowe brothers—he assumed these were two of them—would kill their own mother for a five-cent cigar. Even Fargo, who had faced evil in all of its forms, shuddered inwardly at the nameless depravity in the gunman's flat eyes.

"Bradford," Stone said in a voice that brooked no defiance,

"holster that shooter and come down off your hind legs. How can we turn a profit if you kill all the customers?"

Stone Winslowe aimed his augurlike gaze into Fargo again. "Well, the hell you say! A Bible-thumper . . . Now, that's something to conjure with way out here."

"It's a load of goat shit, Stone," Bradford protested. "Lookit that Arkansas toothpick in his boot. If that bastard's a preacher, I'll eat my six-shooter. Matter fact, these are the same two I saw—"

"Put a sock in it," Stone ordered.

"This knife," Fargo explained mildly, "is more of a tool than a weapon—good for skinning rabbits, softening bed ground and such. This Colt I never use except for killing snakes. I also have a rifle, but I use it only for hunting or in self-defense. Such as yesterday."

Fargo had caught Bradford's slip just now and knew that one of these men might recognize him from yesterday. So it had to be dealt with quick.

"The hell happened yesterday?" Stone demanded.

"That's not too clear, brother Stone, but it looks like renegade Indians attacked and killed three teamsters east of here. Then, as Father and I prepared to give them a Christian burial, the same Indians must have opened fire on us. I fired back, and they cleared out."

Stone Winslowe's face had hardened, eyes narrowing to slits, when Fargo had alluded to the incident. Now it relaxed.

Fargo risked a quick peek at the woman. Her pretty, fine-boned face watched him back, and each time she blinked Fargo couldn't miss the long-lashed eyelids. She wore a stylish straw hat trimmed with blue ribbons and bright ostrich feathers. Fargo didn't buy it—a woman of her obvious high caliber hitched to a stinking brute like Stone Winslowe?

A flat, hard, callused hand abruptly slapped Fargo so hard he staggered sideways.

"Preacher, huh?" Bradford spat out. "You see that, Stone? The man of God was staring at Belinda again."

Sudden rage almost got the better of Fargo, who was not in the habit of letting any man lay a hand upon him. By a supreme effort of will he resisted the urge to burn this bullying bastard down where he stood. Fargo still needed too much information.

The reckoning is coming, Fargo promised himself. *We will be huggin', you tinhorn son of a bitch.*

"A soft answer turneth away wrath, brother Bradford," he replied calmly. "I meant to offend no one."

"What's your name, preacher?" Stone demanded.

"Jacobs. Lemuel Jacobs. This is my father, Jeddediah. We hail from Salt Lake City."

"Mormons, huh? The hell you doing in The Nations?"

"Actually, that's why I came to see you," Fargo replied. "Brother Brigham has permission from the Indian Bureau to build a school of mechanical arts in this area. We hope to teach the Cherokees and other civilized tribes such useful trades as how to operate and repair steam boilers."

Both Winslowe brothers howled with mirth.

"You Indian-loving psalm-singers," Bradford said with contempt, spitting on Fargo's leg. "Tell me, preacher man, you one a them wivin' Mormons? Got you a harem?"

"As a missionary," Fargo replied, "I'm not yet allowed to marry."

"Ahh . . . no wonder you're staring at Belinda, you milk-livered God-monger. You won't find tits like hers on them dried-up hags in Salt Lake."

"Bradford," Stone cut in, "you flap your mouth too much."

The owner looked at Fargo. "*I'm* the rainmaker around here, preacher. Nobody so much as takes a piss without my say-so. If you plan on doing 'God's work,' seek *my* blessing first. That means you sweeten the kitty."

"I'm not a trouble-seeking man, Mr. Stone. As I said, that's why I'm here. You see, the church houses in Salt Lake will be sending gold to Father and me as soon as we've picked a site for our school. But we need to have some place where it can be delivered."

The sneer left Bradford's face. "Gold? How much?"

"That depends on the generosity of the Saints in Salt Lake, but perhaps one thousand dollars to start with."

Again the brothers exchanged glances. Stone noticed that Belinda had been steadily watching Fargo.

"Go scrape the gravy skillet, woman," he snapped at her. "My belly's pinched."

From the corner of one eye, Fargo saw Belinda quickly dry a

tear with a fold of her dress. Equal parts of misery and fear were stamped into her face. She headed toward a door in the back wall—the rest of the cabin was living quarters, Fargo guessed.

The oldest Winslowe brother looked at Fargo again, eyes blazing with greed. "Preacher, how does them church folks in Salt Lake plan to get gold to you out here? All we got is jack-ass mail, and sometimes it takes months just to deliver from Santa Fe."

"We Mormons have started a new fast-messenger service," Fargo lied. "We have relay riders and way stations. The money can get here in two weeks, God willing. It's much easier to find this place than a camp in the wilderness."

"Makes sense," Stone agreed. "Well, we *need* civilization and schools and such out here—more business for me. You go ahead and send it here."

Fargo still had no solid proof the Winslowe brothers had jumped those teamsters. But he knew damn well that any gold sent here would never get delivered. The ruse was designed to buy time—Stone would not have him and Rip killed until he knew that gold was on its way.

"God bless you, brother Stone," Fargo said. "There's a way station just fifty miles west of here. I'll leave word there as soon as Father and I settle a camp."

Outside, the Ovaro gave his trouble whicker. Fargo grabbed Rip's arm and hustled him out the door. They were just in time to see two men—twin brothers, obviously—in the act of trying to lead the Ovaro away.

"H'ar now, you sons of bitches," Rip sputtered until Fargo gave him a sharp jab in the ribs.

"Why, thank you, friends, for unhitching my horse for me," Fargo told them in a hail-fellow-well-met tone. "You must be the other two Winslowe lads."

The "lads" in question each had the same greasy black tangle of hair and hard-bitten, mud-colored eyes that gave no clue to their thoughts. They watched Fargo with the veiled manner of a pair of shifty horse traders. Each man wore two revolvers, and several spare cylinders were tucked behind their sashes.

"Preacher Jacobs," Stone called from the doorway behind him, "these are my kid brothers, Bo and Clint. Bo's the one with the panther scars on his cheek. It's their job to water the customers' horses."

"Then how's come they forgot mine," Rip spoke up, still fuming.

"Oh, we just watered them, thank you," Fargo said, taking the reins from a reluctant Bo. He buckled on the bridle and tightened the saddle cinch, then forked leather.

"Hey, *preacher*!" Bradford shouted, stepping outside and hooking his thumbs behind his shell belt. "What the hell is a meek man of God doing riding an uncut stallion?"

"Brother Bradford, God made him that way, and I don't try to improve on the Lord."

"Shit!" Bradford shouted as the two men rode off. "That 'gold' story of yours might hornswoggle my brother, but it don't fool me. Mister, you best harken and heed—I aim to shoot you to trap bait!"

5

"I'd like to whip that bastard's hide six ways to Sunday," Rip groused as the two horsebackers rode out of the mud hovel.

"Which one?"

"The whole damn litter."

"Christ," Fargo swore, his lips forming a grim slit through his short beard. "I've met plenty of hard twists out west, but *that* bunch takes the prize."

"That was slick work you done," Rip said, "bringing up the 'Indian attack' on the teamsters and how we got pinned down. They done it, all right, and one a them chicken pluckers tried to kill us, too. Happens we'd a kept our mouths shut about it, they woulda guessed we was playin' it foxy and aired us out right in that trading post."

"They pulled that job, all right," Fargo said, his tone musing.

"Well, then, all we had to do was kill 'em and be done with it," Rip fumed. "Tarnation, Fargo, how much damned 'evidence' do you require?"

"More than we have," Fargo insisted. "For one thing, we know at least *five* men jumped those teamsters. Besides, not one of the Winslowe brothers even toted a rifle."

"They're in their home diggin's, that's how's come. That rifle is for special jobs."

Fargo nodded. "You're prob'ly right. But I don't kill a man, Rip, until I got solid proof he needs killing."

"Reckon I can't fault a man for bein' fair—long as fair don't shade over into stupid."

"Point taken. But there's another reason for delaying the showdown—that's no damn trading post, and I mean to find out exactly what's going on around here. This bunch might be part of some bigger operation, and I've got a keelboat behind me that I signed on to protect."

Rip gave him a puzzle-headed look. "Not a trading post? The hell is it—a dance hall?"

"Oh, it *looks* good. But when did you ever see a frontier trading post stocked that full and no customers? Where would any come from? Most white men in The Nations stay holed up, and most of the red men are way up north on reservations scattered around the Arkansas River."

Rip mulled all that. "Fargo, cut off my legs and call me Shorty! All that shines. And, say . . . what kind of 'traders' threaten to kill their customers and try to boost their hosses?"

"It's a poser," Fargo agreed. "And I got a hunch it's all connected to those missing keelboats Etienne mentioned. Don't forget Justin Halfpenny—he knows plenty, but he's too scared to let it out. And that woman Belinda—she should be on a theater stage in San Francisco, not sharing a bed with the likes of Stone Winslowe."

"Somethin' ain't jake there," Rip agreed. "He ain't fit to lace her shoes. She sure was sneakin' peeks at you, though. I do b'lieve she's cocked her eye at you. Too damn bad she's surrounded by snarling curs—plenty of sugar in *them* britches."

"She's top shelf, right enough. But there's always ways to get around curs."

Rip stared at his companion. "You got brain fever? You even go near her, them four brothers will put you with your ancestors."

"The woman's in trouble, old son. That's plain as bedbugs on a clean sheet. On the frontier, it's a man's duty to help her out."

"Ahuh. And I'd wager it's his duty to get underneath her petticoats, too, huh, *preacher*?"

Fargo looked pious. "Lord willing, brother Rip, Lord willing."

For more than an hour, playing a hunch, Fargo had hidden in a clump of red plum bushes along the north bank of Red River.

Knowing a woman as clean and fresh looking as Belinda must bathe often, he had found the most likely spot: a tree-sheltered backwater of the river, a natural bathing pool about fifty yards

35

behind the trading-post compound. A well-worn path down to the river was his best clue, and judging from the stench and appearance of the Winslowe brothers, *their* feet hadn't worn it.

The day had been unseasonably hot, but was cooling now as a big orange disk of sun began settling in the west. Fargo had crept here on foot from a cold camp about a mile downriver, and in case the river became his only escape route, he had left his hat, weapons, and boots behind, slipping on a pair of elk-skin moccasins for easier swimming.

He was on the verge of giving up when a door in the log wall creaked open. The shapely woman, a rough towel of homespun cloth in one hand, a lump of yellowish lye soap in the other, started down the path. She moved with catlike grace—a fluid, seamless motion that ignited a stirring in Fargo's buckskins.

When she unbuttoned her shoes and began undoing the stays of her taffeta dress, Fargo knew he should be a gentleman and announce his presence. But she might, he hastily convinced himself, run away in panic—something a naked woman was unlikely to do. Thus reassured that he had no choice in the matter, Fargo settled in to enjoy the show.

A show he would long remember. Dress, petticoat, and frilly pantaloons were dropped into a pile, revealing a pale, naked goddess. Her legs were slender and shapely, from the well-turned ankles to the supple ivory-smooth thighs. A thatch of dark blond mons hair, looking soft as pure French wool, led up to a creamy stomach with just the right amount of feminine curvature.

When Fargo's eyes made it up to her stunning breasts—hard and heavy, capped with plum-colored aureoles and pink, pointy nipples—he was forced to quell his excited breathing lest she hear him.

She turned to wade into the pool, and Fargo admired a high-split rear that made him think of peaches and cream. With each step, the taut cheeks tightened into perfect concaves.

He waited until she had ducked under to wet her entire body. The moment her head popped out, wheat-blond curls plastered to it like a helmet, he spoke up.

"Don't be frightened, Belinda. I'm a friend and I'm here to help you."

Fargo heard a sharp, hissing intake of breath.

"*Don't* scream," he warned. "That bunch will kill both of us."

His point seemed to sink in. She fisted water from her eyes, seeking him out. "I guess if you were a rapist," she admitted, "you wouldn't have called out. Well, are your eyes closed, at least?"

"No, ma'am. I don't have that much willpower."

This coaxed a small smile from her. "That's an honest answer, and thank you for the compliment. But where are you? *Who* are you?"

She huddled so that only her head and shoulders protruded from the pool. Making sure he wasn't visible from the compound, Fargo stepped into view.

"You," she said, her voice surprised. "A supposed preacher, and I'll bet you watched me undress?"

"Every tantalizing second," he confessed.

"I knew you were no preacher the moment I laid eyes on you."

"And I knew that no woman with your looks and bearing could be a wife to garbage like Stone Winslowe. You're his prisoner, aren't you?"

"I . . . What's your real name, mister?"

"Fargo. Skye Fargo, but keep that dark for both our sakes."

"Skye . . . that's a lovely name. Well, Skye, I advise you to clear out of this region. You don't know how fortunate you were today. One time a man smiled too long at me, and Stone beat him so hard with an axe handle he crippled him for life."

"I've met his kind before. Remember, little tin gods crumple."

She rose farther out of the water, crossing her arms over her breasts. "You look like a capable man, all right. But all four of those brothers are ruthless killers, especially Bradford. He's always bragging that he knows fifty ways to kill a man before breakfast."

"Sounds like it's best to catch him at suppertime," Fargo joked.

"Skye, it's no laughing matter—they're *all* terribly dangerous."

"I know that, Belinda, but I wasn't born in the woods to be scared by an owl. This isn't just about you—those Winslowes have got a reckoning coming. I mean to plant all four of 'em just as soon as I get all the facts I need."

For a moment hope sparked in her eyes. Her arms dropped to her side, and she let his hungry eyes look all they wanted to.

"I think you mean it," she said. "And if I've ever laid eyes on a man who could do it, it's you. Oh, Skye, we were warned, when we left Ohio, about uncouth frontiersmen. But this bunch goes far beyond uncouth."

"We?" Fargo pressed.

"Oh, I *can't* say anything—I dare not."

She boldly walked out of the pool, shivering slightly as the early evening breeze raised gooseflesh on her wet skin and stiffened her nipples into hard tips. "Skye, right now I just want to stop thinking. *Please* help me do that."

Fargo specialized in taking women's minds off their troubles, and this poor lass needed his skills as badly as any. He lifted his shirt and pulled her into him hard, those gorgeous tits grinding into his chest. She kissed him with greedy passion, her tongue a finger exploring his mouth.

Fargo laid her down in the soft spring grass and sucked and nibbled on her pliant nipples as he dropped his trousers, then positioned himself between her spread-open thighs. The chamois-soft folds and petals of her sex glistened with desire.

"My stars, *look* at you!" she exclaimed, catching sight of Fargo's hard, purple-domed manhood, which leaped with each pounding heartbeat. "I thought only a stallion could be that big."

Unable to resist, she gripped it in one hand, marveling as she stroked its length. Fargo felt hot, tingling pinpricks of explosive pleasure already welling in his groin.

"Careful, honey, it's been a while," he warned. "Let's save it for the main event."

"Let me," she begged, bending his staff to the perfect angle and then gasping with carnal pleasure as Fargo thrust his hips forward, plunging into her. Her butt wiggled rapidly in the grass as she squeezed him with her love muscles, teasing him.

Fargo knew he couldn't hold off long with this hot little firecracker, so he pleasured both of them in long, fast strokes, building up a quick head of steam that soon had her climaxing in hard, rapid spasms, crying out against his hard chest to mute the sound. Moments later Fargo's body seemed to come unwired as he thrashed in a powerful release that brought her back over the peak again with him.

For some time both lay dazed by pleasure, not a worry—or even a thought—in the world. Then, like feeling slowly returning to a limb that had gone asleep, the dangerous reality of their situation descended on both of them. Belinda hurriedly started dressing.

"Why can't you tell me more about this mess you're in?" Fargo asked her as he tied his buckskin trousers closed. "You're not married to Stone, are you?"

"Skye, *please* don't ask. It has nothing to do with me. If you ever do kill those . . . monsters, I'll tell you everything. But I dare not breathe a word. And if I run away . . . Well, that's utterly impossible."

Fargo nodded. "Fair enough. You're a woman caught in one mighty rough bind, I see that. But can you tell me anything about what those four are up to? This trading post, it—"

"Belinda!"

Fargo almost jumped out of his skin. The hoarse shout came from dangerously nearby. He glanced through the trees and saw Stone Winslowe advancing, now almost halfway to the pool. A scattergun was tucked under one arm.

"Goddamn it, woman, you want to scrub that lily-white hide right off? Get up here and knock us up some grub, or I'll lay a blacksnake across that high-toned ass of yours!"

Fargo tossed Belinda a two-fingered salute and moved quickly toward the river, snapping off a breathing reed as he waded quietly in. Numerous escapes from Indians had taught him the value of perfecting underwater swimming, and he slipped quietly under the surface, letting the fast current pull him out to midstream.

The current carried him effortlessly, and every minute or so Fargo rolled onto his back to breathe through the reed. When he calculated that he was far enough away, he started to kick toward the surface. But the last slanting beams of dying sunlight illuminated something below.

Fargo took a breath, then dived straight down. The dark shape that had caught his eye, he finally realized, was the badly charred prow of a keelboat, weighted down with boulders.

A gleaming object lay in the murky river bed beside it. Fargo pulled it out of the mud, then felt his blood turn to ice when he realized the object grinning at him was a human skull!

6

"Fargo, you keep goin' back to that post, and you're a done-for case. The way things stand around here, that filly is chain lightnin'."

"Most of the pretty ones are, especially out west."

"Ahuh, and the *married* ones anyplace."

"Don't be too sure she's married, Rip."

"Hell, she's got a weddin' band."

"Yeah, and I was almost murdered once by a wanted criminal wearing a stolen sheriff's badge."

"I take your drift. Anyhow, ask me, a weddin' ring is just like a tourniquet—it prevents circulation."

Fargo had returned to their less-than-ideal camp in a small copse of jack pine near the river. Devoid of graze, it was located in the lee of a wind-scrubbed knoll and at least afforded some screening of their horses if they were kept hobbled.

"Messin' with Stone Winslowe's woman," Rip persisted, "would make even a mule stop and think twice."

"You old lunkhead," Fargo snapped. "If I hadn't gone to see her, I never would've discovered that scuttled keelboat."

"There's that," Rip conceded, munching on a handful of parched corn. "Anyhow, happens she's a prisoner there, like you say, it's a mortal shame. A woman can't run away on her own in country like this. But, say—why can't we bust her loose?"

"We could, but I doubt she'd go, and I won't force her."

Without a fire it was too dark to see well, but Fargo could feel Rip frowning. "She won't go? Why the hell not?"

"I don't know," Fargo admitted, "but I aim to puzzle it out. She'd be safer in a grizzly's den than trapped among those Winslowe brothers."

"Won't go," Rip repeated, wonder in his tone. "I'm damned if I can read sign on the breast of a woman."

Her words from earlier cankered at Fargo: *Skye, it's no laughing matter—they're* all *terribly dangerous.*

"You been wantin' proof agin them killers," Rip's voice sliced into his thoughts. "Well, that sunk keelboat you seen is right in their backyard."

"It sure's hell is, and I'd lay high odds they did it. Problem is, it's not proof you can pick up and put in your parfleche. The two keelboats Etienne said have gone missing disappeared in the past six months. Even with a fast current scouring it, I don't think a skeleton would be as clean as this one. That boat went down some time ago."

"I still think they done it. Who knows how long them puke pails been out here? Then again, back Missouri way, the talk is how it's Comanches or Cherokees done for them two boats. Happens that's so, could be they jumped the one you seen, too."

"Comanches or Cherokees?" Fargo said, his tone skeptical.

"Ain't sayin' I believe it, especially of the Cherokees. But saloon talk says they loaded the goods on travois and traded 'em to Comancheros in New Mexico."

"Sheep dip," Fargo scoffed. "Traded them for what? The only trade goods renegade Indians want are weapons, ammo, and liquor, and that made up most of the supplies on these boats."

"They could pull that out and, happens they was Comanches, trade the rest for slaves and torture victims. To a Comanche, a three-day torture session is better'n a tent revival."

Fargo mulled that. "Good point. But it weakens your case against the Winslowe brothers."

"You're the one calling it a 'case,' Mr. Philadelphia lawyer. I still say we shoulda bored all four of 'em right through their lights while we had the murderin' bastards in one place."

"Easier said than done. Bradford had his palm resting on the butt of that Remington, and the holster ain't oiled to preserve the leather."

"Ahuh, that shines." Rip crunched another mouthful of corn. "I seen that look in your eyes, Fargo, when that jackal slapped you. You mean to throw a gun on him?"

"Rip, it's summary law out here. The hell you *think* I mean to do—powder his butt and tuck him in? The point is when, not what. And it'll be fair. I give every man an even draw. I'll tolerate mild insults, but I won't be laid a hand upon."

"I ain't so sure that 'even draw' business is a smart idea, Fargo. He looks like one a them gunslicks what practices in a mirror all day."

"He's a hard shell, all right. But did you ever see a mirror that shoots back?"

Rip chuckled. "For a fact I have not. Damn it, this parched corn and cold river water leaves a man's backbone scraping his ribs."

"Go easy on it," Fargo advised. "The horses need more now that they can't graze."

"I wish we had us somethin' to cook. When I was a hash-slinger in Sedalia, I was famous for my eggs and scrapple. Let's snare a rabbit."

"And eat it raw? I told you this spot is too open to risk a fire. Do I need to remind a Texas Ranger that Comanches are one of the few tribes who leave their camp circles to raid after dark?"

"No, I recollect that," Rip said. "I also recollect eating prairie rats a few times—this corn ain't so bad at that."

A few minutes passed in silence, Fargo listening to the mournful soughing of the wind in the pines. Something occurred to him.

"You know, Rip, while I was waiting for Belinda, not one customer came to that trading post."

"Ahuh. 'Pears to me they ain't exactly doing a land-office business. But like we was sayin', goods sell high all over the Far West."

"And how," Fargo agreed. "A place settles up quick once there's a gold or silver strike. Just this year Nevada became a territory, all because of the Comstock Lode. I watched a tenderfoot pay one hundred dollars for a barrel of flour with weevils in it."

"Plenty of mazuma in it for them Winslowe skunks," Rip insisted. "They're stealing big shipments, on land and river, and sending them west."

"Well, there's one thing for sure: there's been some high old goings-on hereabouts. The stumper is, exactly who's behind it?"

"God's garters!" Rip exclaimed in exasperation. "Fargo, you're enough to vex a saint. Hell, a man could figure it out on the back of an envelope. It's them sage rats at the trading post. They murdered them three teamsters, amongst others, and tried to kill us. How much 'proof' you need?"

"Oh, they're guilty, all right," Fargo agreed. "But of all the crimes or just some? Could there be another gang, or renegades, working the same deal? And just who is receiving the stolen goods out west? Knowing the Winslowes are in this ain't enough. It's certainty that counts, and this deal still falls short of certain."

"Like I said, I ain't the boy for sagebrush lawyers, but I can't fault a man for bein' fair. Me, I'm a hotheaded Texican, and I say let's just swoop in and plug all four of 'em."

"There's more than four," Fargo reminded him. "At least one more man drove that wagon. How do we nab any accomplices if we kill the Winslowe brothers too soon?"

"You got a good point, and I'm caught upon it. But them sons of bitches is guilty as Judas, and that's a fact."

"You wouldn't know a fact from a hole in your head, you trigger-happy old goat."

Rip waved this aside. "Mebbe not, but I'll *have* a hole in my head if you keep gatherin' them facts."

"We'll sift this matter to the bottom," Fargo promised. "And once it's sifted, we'll put paid to it."

"Mighty tough talk comin' from a 'preacher.' Fargo, you're trickier than a redheaded woman. I like to died when you come up with *that* cowplop. But it was a good grift, at that. Stone won't likely want us killed until after that Indian-school money is sent."

"Might've bought us some time," Fargo agreed. "But that damn Bradford is kill crazy. It's gonna get hot, old son. Lead *will* fly."

"Don't scare me none. *This* child has stopped enough lead to open a smelter. Say, now you're a preacher and all, here's one for you: how do you punish a man who farts in church?"

"You tell me."

"Why, you make him sit in his own pew."

Rip, always the best audience for his own jokes, shook with mirth. Fargo heard liquid sloshing. He reached out and plucked the bottle of rum from Rip's hand.

"You've spent enough time with O. B. Joyful tonight. I don't want you dead drunk on guard duty if those Comanches decide to visit."

"Guard duty?"

"We better. Every two hours we'll do turnabout."

"Makes sense," Rip agreed. "Comanches are night raiders, and like you said, this is their home range even if they don't abide by the treaty."

"Take first watch," Fargo told him, rolling into his blanket and settling his head into the bow of his saddle. "Those boys play rough, so expect trouble to cross our trail at any moment."

The Ovaro gave a warning whicker, and Fargo's eyelids snapped open.

Silver-white moonlight limned everything in a ghostly aura. From the position of the polestar, Fargo guessed it was a couple of hours before dawn—still Rip's second watch.

The Ovaro was quiet now. Maybe, Fargo figured, a rabbit or a coyote had set him off. Both were plentiful around here. Still, Fargo had not survived all these years on the frontier by assuming the best.

"Rip?" he called out quietly, just to make sure.

Instead of the expected response, Fargo detected a wheezing snore. Just then a twig snapped on his left, and survival instinct made him roll fast to the right. A fractional second later, a stone war club smashed into the saddle where his head had just been.

Unfortunately, Fargo had also rolled beyond the spot where his firearms lay, and the Comanche brave leaped on him, black obsidian knife gleaming in the moonlight as he thrust it down, aiming for vitals. In the nick of time Fargo stopped the blade with a forearm block.

For the next few frantic moments, fighting for his life, Fargo had no wind to spare for waking up Rip. The attacker was strong and swift, well versed in ground fighting, and he had his victim in a literal death grip. Fargo held on to the brave's right wrist for dear life, controlling the knife, but the determined warrior gouged at Fargo's eyes with the fingers of his left hand.

They rolled in a confused tangle of limbs, the brave tenacious, Fargo determined. He could smell the musty bear grease in the Comanche's hair. Finally the Trailsman got his knees between the two of them and tossed his assailant free just long enough to jerk the Arkansas toothpick from his boot. This time, when the brave leaped on him, he impaled himself on ten inches of cold, lethally honed steel.

44

The blade sliced through skin, tissue, and muscle, puncturing the brave low in his guts, and Fargo felt body heat wash over his hand. He knew the stab was fatal, and so did the Comanche—his eerie death song, high-pitched and warbling, panicked the Ovaro and Rip's Indian scrub.

Rip, startled awake, shouted, "Here's the elephant!" and discharged his booming Colt's dragoon, a sound like a small cannon. Only then, as several unshod horses took flight in the darkness, did Fargo realize other braves had been waiting nearby.

"You stupid son of a bitch," Fargo cursed when Rip stumbled back into camp, stinking of rum. "I didn't expect a damn thing from you, and by God, you came through."

"Now, Fargo, I—"

"Save it for your memoirs. You got drunk and fell asleep on guard. That would get you shot in the army."

"Fargo, my hand to God! I only had a nip to wash my teeth, and I wasn't asleep, just resting my—"

"Sew up your lips, you pathetic old fool. Ranger, my ass. 'I'm your boy, Fargo, when the war whoop sounds.' You damn near got me killed, and now I've sent a Comanche under."

Fargo pulled a phosphor from his possibles bag, struck it to life with his thumbnail, and held it over the dead brave's face. He swore out loud, a string of foul and creative epithets that would have made a stable sergeant blush.

"It's the same brave that counted coup on me at the river."

"Still grippin' his knife, Fargo, you son of thunder! He was fixin' to split you from scalp to toenails."

"Oh, I won the huggin' match. But sometimes you dodge a flood only to step into a stampede. See those notchings on his bone breastplate?"

Rip squinted, then whistled. "God-in-whirlwinds! You done for a war chief."

"The way you say. Up to now we were just chicken-fixin's to them. *Now* they'll roast our hearts. If they catch us flat-footed again, we're under. Old son, we're in it up to the hubs now."

"We best clear out pretty pronto and find us another camp."

The phosphor burned his fingers and Fargo shook it out.

"We'll never get them Winslowe brothers planted," Rip said, thinking out loud, "withouten we get the Comanches off our tails."

Fargo wiped the blade of his knife on the dead brave's buckskin leg bands. "There's one thing we can do that might help. All the Plains tribes place great store by respectful treatment of their dead. We're going to make this war chief a funeral scaffold."

"You told me you don't bury any man who tries to kill you."

"This ain't burying, Rip. And I'll bend any rule if it means saving my topknot."

"Well," Rip said, "the bastard had a set of oysters on him, for a fact. Let's lay him out."

Using his Arkansas toothpick, Fargo cut and trimmed four strong saplings, carving points on one end of each. With a rope frame and a bed of branches, they laid the body on it with eyes pointed toward the Place Beyond the Sun.

"All right," Fargo said. "Let's saddle up and make tracks. Rip, any man can be brave when the odds are with him. But the odds don't favor us. You can cut and ride now, if you want. Go hole up in your cave again and swill liquor."

"Cowards to the rear, huh?"

"I never called you a coward," Fargo objected.

"Mebbe I got drunk tonight, but it ain't my way to show yellow. Hell, I was in the Runaway Scrape back in 'thirty-six, when General Sam Houston ordered all of us to run from that greasy bastard Santa Anna. Never again—a *dog* might return to his own puke, but not Rip Miller."

Fargo was silent, still debating.

"Hell," Rip wheedled, "by shootin' off my dragoon, I scairt the rest off, am I right?"

Fargo reluctantly nodded. "All right," he said, picking up his saddle, "I'll give you one more chance. But I don't chew my cabbage twice—you fall asleep on guard duty one more time, I'll kill you for cause. We're up against it, Rip, and it's only going to get worse."

7

Sunrise was only two hours away, and both men were too nerve-jangled from the attack to sleep. So instead of making another camp, they rode upriver until they discovered a place where the north bank had caved in, forming a natural dugout. Backs to the dirt wall, weapons to hand, they waited for sunrise.

"Fargo," Rip said as he whittled on a stick, "that sunk keelboat you seen—how do you figure it happened?"

"That's got me treed, Rip. There was a gang of river pirates operating out in California back in 'fifty-five, attacking keelboats along the Salinas River. They'd run a strong rope across the river, about two feet under the surface. When the boat stopped, all hands came out to free the snag. The gang would open up and kill every last one of them before they could break out their weapons."

"Son of a bitch! So then they unloaded the supplies and set fire to the boat?"

"First," Fargo corrected him, "they busted up the boat with a few six-pound cannonballs. Made it easier to sink."

"Say . . . that boat you seen was all busted up, too, hey?"

Fargo nodded. "I'm thinking the same thing you are—this *could* be that same gang. They were run out by vigilantes from the gold fields, but never caught."

Rip mulled something over. "You think just four or five men could do all that? Crews on a keelboat can number as much as twenty men."

"Surprise is the key, and don't forget that voyageurs are piss-poor with firearms."

"That shines. But the killing of the crew would still have to be did quick."

Fargo nodded. "Way I figure it, these Winslowe brothers only need one extra man—a teamster—when they hit freight wagons. But they prob'ly hire on extra guns for the keelboats."

"Sure, and look at that hovel what sprung up next to the phony tradin' post—priddy near every swingin' dick in a hellhole like that is likely outlaws on the dodge. 'Specially here in The Nations."

"However it's playing out," Fargo said, "we have to protect any new boats coming along *and* figure out where those supplies are going. And if there is a cannon, we have to find it."

"Sounds like you finally got all the proof you require," Rip put in.

"Not enough yet to kill those four bastards," Fargo said. "But I'm almost there."

"You *still* think it could be renegade Injins doin' this?"

Fargo shook his head. "It's white men. Indians despise hard labor and wouldn't clean out all the supplies—heavy barrels and so forth. They have to travel light and fast, and they'd take only what they could use."

Twenty or so minutes passed in silence between them while Red River chuckled and the eastern sky began to show the first salmon pink streaks of dawn.

"That little cottontail," Rip said. "What's her front name—Linda?"

"Belinda."

Rip grunted. "Pretty name for a pretty girl. You don't spoze all four of them brothers is—"

"Sew up your lips, old fart. A man doesn't have to speak *every* thought that comes into his head."

Rip snorted. "Sheer, spiteful cussedness—that's me."

Fargo watched the sun finally edge over the eastern horizon. "All right, sheer cussedness, let's tack up and head upriver. We need a good campsite with plenty of tree cover and good graze. We're low on corn."

"Then what? Back to the trading post to tell 'em that gold's on its way from Salt Lake?"

"It's too soon," Fargo said, throwing his saddle on and centering it. "They won't believe me. Remember, I'm supposed to be riding to a way station fifty miles west. We'll wait at least one more day."

"Say, Fargo, I just thought of this. Wunst we tell them thievin' bastards the gold's on its way, what keeps them from fillin' us with lead?"

"Not one damn thing, that's what. So when we go in there, we're gonna make sure *we* open the ball. I've worn this 'preacher' story out, anyhow, so we'll just put our cards on the table."

"That's the gait! All they can do is kill us. When we do ride back, what about that jasper workin' the smithy? Justin who-sis?"

"Justin Halfpenny. Yeah, we need to talk to him some more. He knows a lot more than he's letting on."

"So does that little filly Belinda, to hear you tell it. But both of 'em is scairt spitless."

"I won't press her," Fargo replied. "She's protecting somebody and she won't talk out even if she's tortured."

Fargo sheathed his Henry and slipped the riding thong over the hammer of his single-action Colt. Then he gave the cinches and latigos one last tug before he grabbed a fistful of mane and stepped up into leather.

The morning air was crisp, and a steady northerly wind chilled Fargo through his buckskins as the two riders followed the meandering Red River due west. About an hour after sunrise, Fargo's distance-trained eyes spotted two figures well out ahead, wading in and out of the river.

He broke out his brass field glasses and studied them.

"I can't make out their faces," he reported to Rip. "A sorrel and a claybank are hobbled on the bank. But there's a Spencer carbine—no, a rifle—sticking out of the saddle scabbard on the sorrel, and a scope mounted on it. You ever see any Spencer with a visible magazine?"

"Never. You load a Spencer through a trap in the butt plate. Holds seven rounds."

Fargo nodded, lowering the glasses. "Exactly. I'd guess that magazine holds twice that. And seeing how the piece has obviously been modified at a gun shop or even the factory, it could have been bored and rechambered for bigger slugs."

"The same damn hand cannon that almost done for us."

"Seems likely. Play it frosty, Rip."

Fifteen minutes later the two horsebackers were close enough to recognize the twin brothers, Bo and Clint Winslowe.

"The *hell* they doin'?" Rip muttered. "Ain't no fool ever

panned for gold in the Red River. For gold, has to be mountains close by."

"Gold comes in many forms," Fargo reminded him. "Hold your powder unless they commence to shooting."

By now the two men, knee-deep in a swirling current, were watching the riders approach, cocky sneers on their faces. All of these Winslowe brothers—especially Bradford, the gunslinger—exuded a self-satisfied manner that irritated Fargo to the point of wanting to wipe that smugness right off their maps.

"Brother Bo, Brother Clint," Fargo greeted them pleasantly. "Looks like you gents forgot your fishing poles."

"Kiss my hairy white ass, preacher man," Bo retorted, following his brother back up onto the bank. As before, both men were heeled with two revolvers and several spare cylinders. They also wore cruel, long-roweled spurs of Mexican silver, explaining their mounts' deeply scarred flanks.

"Yeah, tell us something, holy man," Clint said. "Just exactly how does a virgin pop a baby out? That one gets my money."

"You boys are blasphemers," Fargo said. "That's a sure way to spend eternity shoveling coal in hell."

"Shovel a cat's tail," Bo snapped, his panther-scarred cheek livid in the new sunlight. "The hell you doing following us?"

"You're a mite edgy," Fargo protested. "If we were following you, would we ride right up on you? We're merely riding to the way station at Leonville to leave a message about the gold delivery."

"For your *school*, right?" Clint tossed in.

"Lord willing, yes. Good day, gentlemen."

"Hold up!" Bo exclaimed. "That's a damn fine stallion you're riding, preacher. Lemme fork him and try his mettle."

"Sorry, brother Bo. I don't loan out my horse."

"Shut pan, you lanky bastard, or I'll lay you out."

Fargo's lips formed a grim, determined slit. "Even a preacher need not abide death threats. Now stand clear."

"That's cemetery talk," Bo warned him.

"Damn straight it is, you mouthy pup," Rip spoke up, resting his hand on the big walnut butt of his dragoon pistol.

"I said give over," Bo growled, grabbing the Ovaro's halter.

Touching his horse tore it for Fargo. Tasting the acidic bile of rage, he drew his left foot from the stirrup and smashed

Bo across the mouth with it, sending the man cartwheeling backward until he stumbled. But Fargo's dander was up and he didn't stop there, swinging down to pounce on the man where he lay.

Clint went for one of his revolvers, but the low metallic click of Rip's hammer being thumb-cocked froze him in place.

"Jerk it if you're game, Winslowe," he invited. "But I'll blow you across the River Jordan."

"You old tub of guts, the worm will turn. And then I'll feed your asshole to your liver."

"Caulk up, you scurvy-ridden whoreson! My boy is the preacher, not me. *This* child don't turn the other cheek. Just mind your pints and quarts, or you'll be gettin' your mail delivered by moles."

Fargo, meantime, was venting his fury on Bo Winslowe. Straddling the man's chest to pin him, Fargo rained a series of numbing one-two punches on the stunned miscreant. Blood, and shards of broken, rotten tooth, sprayed in both directions, and Fargo split both lips until they looked like raw meat.

Clint Winslowe, red with fury, again dropped a hand toward one of his holsters.

"Happens that shooter clears leather, boy," Rip warned in a lethal tone, "I'll sink an air shaft through you."

"You wait and see, you toothless old geezer—that stallion *will* be ours."

"Ahuh. And every Jack shall have his Jill, too."

Fargo, exhausting his rage, finally stood up. Bo had been beaten senseless.

"You killed him, you son of a bitch!" Clint shouted.

"He'll come sassy again," Fargo said. "In a few hours. But I'm not in the mood right now, Winslowe, to calibrate insults. I'll give you five seconds to apologize for calling me a son of a bitch, or you'll be stretched out beside your brother."

"I take it back," Clint hastened to say, though reluctantly.

Fargo walked over toward him, and Clint flinched back. But Fargo merely pulled both Remingtons from their holsters and chucked them into the middle of the river. He did the same with Bo's guns and ammo and the magazine from the modified Spencer rifle.

By now Clint was livid with rage, though he avoided any personal insults. "You better hunt a hole, both of you! You're worm fodder now! You never leave a man on the frontier without weapons."

"Simmer down," Fargo advised him. "You can fish the guns and ammo out and dry all of it off. I just want time to ride out of back-shooting range."

"You made a big mistake, preacher. Bo holds a grudge until it hollers mama. You best get right with that God of yours because you just brought down the thunder."

"Thunder never killed a man, brother Clint," Fargo said mildly as he forked leather. "Your brother started this—you never touch another man's horse without his say-so. By law, I *could* have killed him for a horse thief."

"Law? There ain't no law in The Nations."

Fargo stared so long at the other man that he fidgeted. "That's right, *brother* Clint, there ain't. So I plan to make it as I go. You're just lucky that I believe in mercy."

"*Mercy?* Christ, look at his face."

Fargo gigged the Ovaro forward. "Just look at it as a blessing. Now nobody will stare at his panther scars."

The two men had ridden west for perhaps fifteen minutes when Rip demanded, "Fargo, why in tarnal hell are you grinning?"

"Why not? A good set-to always gets my blood singing."

Rip shook his head. "Boy, you musta been conked hard on the noggin when you was a tadpole."

"And you're just an old calamity howler."

Rip, too, suddenly grinned. "God dawg! Fargo, you beat that surly bastard like a rented mule. Trouble is, looks like your 'preacher' grift has gone to smash."

Fargo slued around in the saddle and studied their backtrail before he answered. "It's a sticker, all right, but maybe not. There's preachers who can use their fists, especially west of the Missouri. Stone is a greedy bastard, and he wants that gold."

"Ahuh, but Bo won't care a frog's fat ass—he'll powderburn you first chance he gets."

"Won't be the first man who tried to put me six feet closer to hell—nor the last, I'll wager. Besides, I whaled the snot out of him. He'll be stove up for at least two days."

"That shines. So if we ride in there tomorrow, we should be shut of him. It's that damn Bradford gives me the fantods."

"He's a mad dog," Fargo agreed. "And I didn't fool him with the Mormon preacher story. He'll bear watching—all of them will."

"But the queer deal is, what was Clint and Bo doin' in the river?"

"I been puzzling that one out," Fargo said. "You'll notice there ain't too many solid trees growing near the water. But that spot where we found them has a big cottonwood on either side."

"God's trousers! They're lookin' to snag a keelboat—maybe even the one you're scoutin' for. Only, they picked a different place this time."

Fargo nodded. The sun burned in earnest now, and he shifted his hat to block it. "If they tie the rope low, then trench it on shore, they could run it under the surface without it showing on the banks. A few stone weights tied to it would hold it down."

"What all's on that boat you scout for?"

"Plenty of guns and black powder, bolts of valuable cloth, coffee, sugar, pig lead for molding bullets, barrels of flour, ready-made boots and some other supplies," Fargo replied.

"Hunh. Everything you just rattled off was in that trading post."

Fargo reined in and stood up in the stirrups to see better. The river formed an oxbow on their left, the brownish yellow plains of north Texas stretching to infinity beyond the Red River Valley. On their right, rolling sand hills and scattered mottes of pine marked the southern reaches of the Indian Territory.

"Them Winslowe boys ain't on our trail," Rip said. "Bo's lucky if he can sit his saddle."

"It's Comanches I'm worried about. By now they know we killed a respected war chief."

"Hell, he jumped you in your bedroll. Ain't like you snuck into his wickiup and raped his squaw. 'Sides, we done what we could to lay his body out respectful-like. Mebbe that smoothed their feathers."

"Anyhow," Fargo said, "I see no sign of them."

Fargo had just resumed his seat in the saddle when a familiar, powerful boom sounded well behind them.

"Christ, it's that big-medicine rifle," Rip fretted. "They plinkin' at us?"

Fargo shook his head. "Too far behind us. C'mon, let's dust our hocks."

They wheeled their mounts and raced back along the river bank, Fargo alert for a trap. Twice he halted and scoured the terrain with his eyes.

"There," he said as they rode out of a bend. A roan with a roached mane was taking off the grass. About twenty feet behind him, an obviously dead Indian lay crumpled in the grass.

"Good God Almighty," Rip muttered. "The top of his head is gone."

"Cherokee," Fargo said. "See that red sash? He was a tribal policeman."

They hobbled their horses well back into the bend, knowing they were tempting targets. Both men moved cautiously forward, seeking cover where they could, Fargo holding his Henry at the ready.

"The hell was he doin' way down at the Texas line?" Rip wondered aloud. "Ain't most of the Cherokees farther north of the river valley?"

Fargo nodded, keeping his slitted blue eyes in constant scanning motion. "I'm damned if I know, Rip, but we need to find out. The agency is about twenty miles north of here. We're going to take the body back."

"Hell, Fargo, I'm sorry he got killed, but it ain't none of our picnic. He ain't no Christian."

"You don't know that, old hoss. Plenty of rez Indians have been converted. And it *is* our picnic if the Winslowes killed him. Besides, Christian or pagan, we can't just let the buzzards bury him. He must have family and clan that will wonder about him."

Rip gave a reluctant nod. "Ahh, you shame me, Fargo. He's a Cherokee, and them's good people."

Averting their eyes from the Cherokee's horribly mutilated head, the two men rolled him up in his slicker and lashed him securely to his horse. They returned to their own mounts and Fargo lashed the roan by a lead line to his saddle horn.

"No point trying to flush the killers," Fargo decided. "They've had plenty of time to raise dust, and we'll just be next in their sights."

"*His* sights, you mean," Rip put in. "Clint Winslowe done this—hell, Bo ain't fit to find his own pizzle after that whippin' you gave him. Tarnation, Fargo, why'n'cha grab that Spencer when you had the chance?"

"I had no call to, that's why. Knowing ain't the same as proving. I'd no sooner take a man's weapons than I would his horse."

"Sheep dip! Us Rangers under Captain Coleman had us a motto when it come to Indians: whip them first, *then* talk of treaties. And that's how it'll have to be with this Winslowe trash."

"You're right about whipping the Winslowes," Fargo replied grimly. "But you can't make treaties with dead men. The final proof will come soon, and then all four of those scum suckers will be going to their last account."

8

Good water was scarce north of the Red River Valley, so before they rode out Fargo filled his goatskin water bag and lashed it behind his cantle. Not wanting to be caught in the open after dark, he gave the Ovaro his head and they settled into an easy lope.

The terrain grew flatter and more open as they headed deeper into The Nations and closer to the Cherokee agency at Lone Grove. Rip's tired eyes, like old wounds, peered out from the weathered grooves of his face. "So far, no sign of them Comanches. Ain't no hiding from them now."

"I prefer this open country," Fargo said. "You don't have to fear ambushes, and you can spot any riders from miles off. Speaking of that . . ."

Fargo hauled back on the reins and swung down, stretching out on the ground with one ear just above it.

"Hear anything?" Rip asked.

Fargo shook his head and hit leather again. "I'd guess those Comanches are mourning their dead war chief. Once that's done, we might be up against it."

At times the grass thinned out, and their mounts' hooves raised yellow plumes of dust. Now and then they passed a struggling Cherokee homestead, mostly plank shacks covered with weathered wagon canvas. A few farmers were busy pulling and burning stumps to clear land for crops, but Fargo knew droughts out here were frequent and there was no source for irrigation. Even when crops did push up, they were at risk from great hordes of grasshoppers.

As if reading his thoughts, Rip said, "They can thank Andy Jackson for this hellhole. He told 'em a reg'lar hoe-man's paradise awaited 'em."

56

Fargo nodded. "The Cherokees still call Jackson 'Sharp Knife' because that's how his lying tongue cut them. Everything they had back east—and they had plenty—was stolen from them. These are good people and they didn't deserve this banishment. This is cattle country, not farmland."

The sun blazed hotter than the hinges of hell, and Fargo tilted his broad-brimmed hat against its progress. Reluctantly, however, he left his canteen alone. One swallow in the shade was better than a quart hogged in the sun, so he waited for the pockets of shade.

At one point they spelled the horses in a small pine copse.

"The hell's them?" Rip asked, pointing to fresh notches carved into a tree.

"Messages from Cherokee couriers," Fargo replied. "But no white man has ever figured out the code."

"Could be about us," Rip conjectured, nodding toward the third horse. "They ain't blind. The recognize that horse, and they must know who's lashed across it."

"Sure they do. The moccasin telegraph is faster than the white man's singing wire. I just hope they don't think we killed him."

"Would Cherokees jump us?" Rip wondered.

Fargo shook his head. "For Indians, they rile cool. But once they get blood in their eyes, they're some pumpkins as warriors."

"Well, you said you helped them out, a few years back, in a scrape agin land-grabbers. Here's hopin' they recollect you."

Another forty-five minutes in the saddle brought them within sight of the Lone Grove Cherokee agency, a solid limestone building with a brush ramada out front. Several Cherokees lounged on a split-log bench outside. Spotting the slicker-wrapped body, however, they quickly dispersed.

"They believe the soul of a dead man," Fargo explained quietly as the two men stripped their saddles and tossed them on the rail out front, "has twenty-four hours to jump into a new body."

A friendly voice from the doorway arrested their attention. "Well, I'll be switched! Skye Fargo!"

A slightly built man with a wild brush of frizzled gray hair and a bookish face stepped outside to greet them.

"Niles Wolcott," Fargo said with a smile. "You're still here after all these years? I figured you were back in Boston lecturing

57

to the blue bloods. This old cuss siding me is Rip Miller, former Texas Ranger."

However, Wolcott's welcoming smile melted like a snowflake on a river when he recognized the horse with the roached mane. "Chato Grayeyes, may he rest in peace. Do you know what happened, Skye?"

"We didn't witness it, but we heard the shot. He was murdered close to Red River. Matter fact, been a lot of killing down in the valley lately."

"Do you know who did it?"

"Sure as sun in the morning," Rip piped up.

"We're pretty sure who did it," Fargo corrected him. "But we have no proof."

"Hang your damn proof," Rip muttered.

Wolcott chuckled. "There's a pump out back, gents, where you can wash off the trail dust. Then come on inside and have some venison stew. I also have some good brandy."

When both men trooped inside, hair still dripping, Wolcott led them into a large front room of pine boards so new they still smelled like trees. A mud chimney rose from a flagstone hearth. A Cherokee housekeeper stirred a pot resting on a cooking tripod.

"Niles, that stew smells mighty good after more than two days of eating parched corn," Fargo assured their host.

"Got anything that kicks a little harder than brandy?" Rip asked, earning a dirty look from Fargo.

"Sorry, Mr. Miller, but strong spirits aren't allowed on Indian reservations."

Both men stuck their legs under a long plank table and the housekeeper served them big pottery bowls of hot stew. Wolcott poured brandy into three pony glasses.

"Chato Grayeyes," Wolcott said, his tone heavy with sadness, "is the second tribal policeman killed investigating that river. He was a good man, Skye. Left a wife and three children who will now be destitute."

"I can guess why you sent him south," Fargo said. "These recent attacks on teamsters and keelboats."

Wolcott nodded, his face a maze of worry lines. "I know my Cherokees had nothing to do with it. I took station here four years ago, Skye, and I can attest these Indians are law-abiding."

"I know that firsthand," Fargo assured the agent. "They fought beside me against Baptiste Menard, that French crook who tried to drive them out and get timber rights over their land. They were fierce warriors, all right, but warriors and criminals are two different animals."

"My point exactly. Back in Washington City, however, 'official' opinion is divided. One faction blames the recent attacks on Cherokees, another says it's renegade Comanches from the Staked Plain of Texas."

"Them blowhards in paper collars back east don't know an Injin from an Arab," Rip put in, juice dribbling down his chin.

"You're right, Mr. Miller, because I used to be one of them," Wolcott said. "Even worse than their ignorance, the Indian Bureau is corrupt at every level, and they favor mass punishment."

"Meaning what?" Fargo asked.

"Meaning if these attacks don't halt soon, *all* annuities to the Indian Territory will be halted, and many of these tribes are going to starve."

"I don't think *any* Indians are behind it," Fargo said. "Not even outside renegades. Indians will attack, sure, but they never clean out the spoils lock, stock, and barrel. All the evidence points to a well-organized white gang."

"I've thought so all along," Wolcott said. "But Indians are always the favorite scapegoats of murderers and thieves. Since they're all 'wild savages,' the public is ready to believe the worst of them."

"Happens you growed up in Texas," Rip put in, "you'd know they ain't all scrubbed angels, neither. You ever seen what Comanches or Pawnees do to white women and children? I seen—"

"Never mind your stump speeches," Fargo cut Rip off impatiently. "We're talking about Cherokees now, Rip, and you know damn well they aren't behind these attacks."

"Never said they was," Rip grumped.

"At any rate," Wolcott resumed, "it's hard enough for these people even when the annuities get through. A typical meal around here these days is a dipper of water and a hard biscuit. I haven't had stew like this in over a month."

Wolcott paused to place a pinch of snuff between cheek and gum, then snapped his silver snuffbox shut. "Skye, just now you mentioned that the evidence points toward a white gang?"

"Have you heard of four bothers named Winslowe?"

"Yes. They run a trading post on Red River. When I first heard about it I rode down there. I presented my credentials and asked to see their U.S. Army merchant's license. They had one, issued out of Fort Sill to Stone Winslowe."

"Issued? The way I hear it," Fargo said, "they're *sold* by a corrupt commanding officer."

"Yes. That would be Colonel Clark Pettigrew, over whom I have no authority. In any event, I've been delighted to discover that Winslowe is not selling guns or liquor to Indians."

"There's a good reason for that, Niles. He's not selling anything to anybody—not here in The Nations, anyhow."

Wolcott looked perplexed. "Come again?"

"When you went down there, did you see any customers in the post?"

"Come to think of it, no."

"And the shelves," Fargo pressed on, "were they well stocked?"

Understanding was dawning in the agent's face. "To overflowing."

"The 'trading post' is a sham so the brothers can possess stolen goods, without having to hide them, until they ship them farther west where they can mark up the prices. The Winslowe gang—probably with some hired help now and then—is behind the attacks on the teamsters and the keelboats."

"You can prove this, Skye?"

"In court? Prob'ly not—yet. But to my own satisfaction, hell yes."

"Where," Wolcott wondered, "are they sending the goods?"

"That one's still a stumper," Fargo admitted. "Anyplace where the markup is sky-high. The California goldfields are about played out, but the Comstock is going great guns. My favorite hunch, though, is Santa Fe—it's a lot closer, and almost every week a merchant caravan loads up on provisions for the trip deep into Mexico."

Wolcott mulled this for a full minute. "Skye, you stand well in these parts, especially after stopping Baptiste Menard from almost stealing much of the reservation. I know my tribal policemen would be proud to work under you."

"Obliged," Fargo said. "I may ask for them. Me and Rip have

been outnumbered from the jump—including by renegade Comanches."

"Yes, they raid constantly."

"That's why," Fargo explained, "I'd like to avoid getting your Cherokees in the mix, if possible. You don't want the Comanches setting up a vengeance pole against your people."

"This wouldn't be charity work," Wolcott assured him. "I have discretionary funds set aside for this serious matter. You two solve this mystery, and I'll pay you two hundred dollars in gold double eagles."

Fargo and Rip exchanged a glance. It wasn't exactly a fortune, but the average laborer in America made one dollar for a twelve-hour workday.

"You hold that money for us, Niles," Fargo told him. "We're going to win the horse or lose the saddle—no half measures."

Belinda Starr's hands trembled so hard that they fumbled as she tried to unbutton her dress.

"Hurry the hell up, you high-toned slut," Stone Winslowe snapped, "or I'll tear that fancy rag right off you."

A fat stub of tallow candle burned on a puncheon table, pushing shadows back into the corners of a cramped bedroom. Stone's face was lighted clearly, and Belinda told herself he was aptly named: a face like a slab of granite, with hard, piercing eyes like a pair of bullets.

The floral print dress finally fell in a puddle at her feet.

"Get them dainties off, too," he ordered. "Then stretch out on that bed."

The bed in question was simply a crude shakedown with a shuck mattress, but as his "wife," Belinda was forced to sleep in it every night. Sometimes she could hear mice rustling around inside, and it ruined her appetite for days.

She slipped off her petticoats and lace pantaloons, face flaming as he stared at her like a starving cur staring at a steak—a steak it was impossible for him to eat, which only fueled his hunger.

Stone never actually smiled. There was just a little pulling of his lips for a second or two. They twitched now. "Damn. Just *damn*! Lookit them nipples. Look just like in 'em French paintings. Just like juicy plums. Oh, you're top-shelf, all right."

A tear of humiliation and sadness trickled down her cheek.

"So it's the waterworks again, huh?" he demanded. "You don't fancy being my wife?"

"*Wife?* Stealing my mother's ring and forcing me to wear it hardly makes us man and wife."

He crossed the room in three long strides and slapped her so hard it left her ears ringing. "Oh, don't *you* fart through silk? You don't like it, fancy piece, you're free to vamoose anytime you like."

Tears choked her voice. "You keep saying that, but we both know what happens if I do."

"It's still a choice, ain't it? You ain't trapped here." Those eyes like lance points devoured her naked body. "You know my brothers live just a stone's throw away. You want I should move them in, too, let 'em take turns bulling you all night long?"

In her sudden anger, she spoke without thinking. "You'd never do that. Then they'd find out you can't—"

Belinda clamped her mouth shut, but not before he caught her meaning. "Can't *what*, you mouthy whore?"

She shook her head. "Nothing."

Growling like a rabid animal, he threw her hard to the bed. "Think you're *some*, don'tcha, with your store-bought words and highfalutin airs. I always wanted me a silky-satin woman, and now I got me one. Now, open them legs wide and say your piece."

Face hot with shame, she spread open her legs. "Take me, Stone. Shove your big, hard manhood in me and ride me hard all night until I'm screaming with pleasure. Oh, you're all man, Stone, and only you can pleasure me the way I need it. You . . ."

A sob choked off her voice. Liquid fear iced her veins when he stalked closer to the bed. At times, such as right now, his voice became a razor-thin whisper, and that was when Belinda feared him the most.

"S'matter? You too fine-haired for such talk?"

"No, Stone," she lied. "I don't mind it."

"Don't bullshit me, girl. You hanker after all them soft-handed bastards back east, the ones that sing psalms and stink of lilac toilet water. *That's* how's come I can't . . . how's come it won't work right. It's you, not me. Hell, I can top a squaw or rut on a two-bit whore anytime I want, y'unnerstan'?"

"Of course, Stone. It's my fault, not yours."

"I'm damned if I'm putting on a topper and swallowtails. Close your damn legs, it ain't gonna happen tonight, either."

Grateful for the reprieve, she pulled a rough horsehair blanket over herself. As he always did after these failures, Stone began nervously pacing the small room.

"I seen you lusting after that tall preacher who come in yesterday," he remarked. "How's come *he* ain't too common for you, huh? Hell, he wears bloody buckskins."

"I wasn't 'lusting' after him. I just thought he was an odd-looking preacher."

"I know 'B' from a bull's foot, you high-toned whore. You got one thing right, though—something about him just don't cipher. You seen what he done to Bo's face this morning. It's all swole up like bees stung him. Ain't no man goes toe-to-toe with Bo and walks away from it. Hell, once I watched Bo beat the living shit out of three soldiers that cheated him at cards. Where would a 'preacher' get that tough?"

Alarm tingled Belinda's blood. She regretted her remark about Skye Fargo being "an odd-looking preacher."

Stone paused, searching his memory. "Seems like I heard something once about a tall man in buckskins who rides a black-and-white stallion."

Belinda had not seen Fargo's horse. Stone's remark just now had triggered a sudden memory of a newspaper story—one about a Western hero called the Trailsman. Her blood sang with elation for the first time in months, and hope swelled within her breast like a tight bubble. Hope, not just for herself, but for those she loved most in the world.

The Trailsman, she told herself. He said he'd be back, but could even a newspaper hero survive the Winslowe brothers?

9

"You know, Fargo," Rip said as the two men rode south the next morning, "I ain't slept in a real bed since I lit a shuck out of Sedalia. I'm glad Wolcott invited us to stay last night. Felt good not havin' to loop a rope around me to keep off the rattlesnakes."

"Yeah, the bed part is all right," Fargo agreed. "But not the walls and ceiling. I like to see stars when I look up."

"That Wolcott, he's a nice enough jasper. But . . . *brandy*? Hell, out west you can't even trust a man who puts water behind his whiskey."

"It did taste a mite like patent medicine," Fargo agreed. "But that's what the genteel folks back in Boston drink."

Fargo kept his slitted gaze in constant motion across the mostly flat, barren terrain. Those renegade Comanches could ride out of the bloodred sun at any moment. Yesterday, he had been bothered by a slight clicking from the Ovaro's rear, offside shoe—a sign it was loose. While at the agency, however, both men had taken the time to trim their horses' feet and nail the shoes back on tight.

"Hey, speaking of Niles Wolcott," Fargo said, "we were his guests, you chucklehead. You didn't need to come butting in there shooting off your chin about killer Indians."

"Why, the hell's fire I did! I only—"

"Bottle it," Fargo said. "You got the manners of a buffalo hider. But I like you, Rip. Don't know why, but I do."

"No need to slop over," Rip said sarcastically. "Say . . . that two hunnert dollars Wolcott mentioned. Happens we put the kibosh on this Winslowe bunch, any chance we'll go snooks on the money?"

Fargo slanted a reproving glance toward him. "Of course we'd share it fifty-fifty. What, you think I'm a thieving Winslowe?"

Rip waved the remark off. "It's just . . . so far, you been pullin' most of the freight."

"We take equal risks of getting killed," Fargo reminded him. "Each man does what he can. Anyhow, no need to be spending money we ain't earned yet. You saw Chato Grayeyes—that could be us, too, if we don't play this deal smart."

"Well, happens we do earn it, will you keep the keelboat job long?"

Fargo grinned. "Nope. I'll take it through to Wichita Falls and then cut loose. I'm overdue for a loafing spell. I never stick with any job very long—guess I've got jackrabbits in my socks."

"People say you seen every nook and cranny of the frontier country," Rip said. "What's your favorite part?"

"Almost all of it," Fargo replied. "But riding down off the Wind River Mountains into South Pass and the Sweetwater Valley is some of the finest country a man could ever see. And you can pull trout out of the Sweetwater with your hands."

"I been up there," Rip boasted. "South Pass—Jim Bridger's gift to the Oregon Trail. I recollect—"

"Pipe down," Fargo interrupted. "This is no Sunday stroll. Keep your eyes skinned for any sign of those Comanches. Right now we've got to get back to that keelboat and get Etienne caught up on these river pirates. It's been nigh on to three days since we rode out, and those voyageurs must be close to mutiny."

"All right, I'll pipe down," Rip promised, "after you answer me one more question. Why'n'cha take up Wolcott on his offer of Cherokee policemen? You yourself said they're good fighters."

"I will if it comes to that, but I meant what I said—if Cherokees have to fight Comanches, it could cause a blood grudge for years. Besides, I don't favor a big group of riders in this open country. The key to survival out here is the element of surprise, and that means not being seen."

By now it was well past midmorning and they were traversing the sandy hills preceding the bluffs that overlooked the Red River Valley. When they reached the lip of the bluffs, Fargo reined in just before the edge. Not wanting to skyline himself for any shooters below, he quickly hobbled the Ovaro foreleg to rear and crept to the edge of the bluff, Rip right behind him.

"Great glory in the morning, Fargo!" Rip exclaimed when he saw the sight below.

The narrow valley was a green oasis in the semiarid terrain surrounding it, and Red River a winding blue-green ribbon brilliant with reflected sunlight. And sailing along it in midstream, square sail billowing with a favoring wind from the east, was a cargo-laden keelboat.

"It ain't Etienne and his bunch, at least," Rip said.

"No, but there's a damn good chance they're sailing into the jaws of death," Fargo replied. "Now I know why we saw Clint and Bo upstream in the river—and right where two trees grew opposite each other. They knew this boat was coming."

"The hell do we do?" Rip demanded.

"I got a couple of plans," Fargo said. "The simplest is to try and warn them right now. These bluffs are steep, but my stallion can walk down a wall, and your mustang has perfect legs for this descent."

"Descent? Right here? Fargo—"

"Never mind. Just ki-yi that mustang over the lip, then loosen the reins and let him take over. He'll likely slide at some point, so hold your stirrups and hang on tight to the horn. But if he starts to tumble, jump clear."

They pulled the hobbles from their mounts, Rip's face white as a fish belly.

"Grab some saddle and get about ten yards to my left!" Fargo barked, forking leather. "And nerve up! These horses will do all the work."

The Ovaro didn't hesitate for a moment when Fargo slapped his rump, horse and rider sailing off the bluff. The stallion's powerful forelegs served as brakes when gravity and the steep angle pulled them faster and faster, gravel and stones streaming with them. At one point Fargo almost pitched forward over the pommel, only his strong legs saving him.

"Jesus Christ with a wooden dick!" Rip bellowed on Fargo's left. "Fargo, you son of a bitch, you've killed me!"

"Open your eyes, you fool," Fargo called back. "We're down."

They were indeed safe and sound at the sandy base of the bluff.

"Ahoy!" Fargo shouted through cupped hands. "Ahoy, the keelboat! Danger ahead, come ashore!"

Just then Fargo realized something was very wrong. Not one man showed on deck or in the plank pilothouse at the bow.

"Rip!" he shouted. "Let's vamoose! They must think we're river pirates trying to trick—"

A dozen rifle muskets suddenly appeared over the low gunnel and fired a booming volley. Lead balls snapped past their heads, and a haze of black-powder smoke drifted over the river.

"My conk cover!" Rip shouted when his slouch hat flew off.

"Leave it!" Fargo shouted, but the stubborn old fool slid off his horse to retrieve it.

"I've had it thirty years, Fargo," he explained as both men raced their horses full tilt east along the riverbank.

They reined in when they were safely out of range.

"Holy Hannah!" Rip exclaimed. "Them boys got a bead on us quicker than an Indian going to crap."

"Good thing for us they don't have repeaters," Fargo said. "I've never yet met a boatman who can shoot worth a damn, and right now I'm glad of it."

"What's the big idea now?" Rip demanded.

"They're sailing against the current. So even if the wind holds steady, it'll take at least two hours for them to reach that ambush point. That gives us plenty of time to talk to Etienne and still beat the boat. C'mon, let's make tracks."

The two riders found a gravel ford about a hundred yards upriver from the anchored keelboat, racing the final distance at a 2:20 clip. Fargo pulled the pinto to his haunches and leaped off, calling for Etienne. The captain of voyageurs, armed with a carbine, hurried down the gangplank to shore.

"Monsieur Fargo," he greeted him. "We can sail now, *non*?"

"'Fraid not," Fargo told him. "There's river pirates upstream."

"They want *this* boat?"

"You can take that to the bank." Fargo assured him. "They don't play favorites."

"These pirates—they are *peaux-rouges*?"

"Forget redskins," Fargo said. "These pirates are all paco-faces."

Etienne wrung his hands like a helpless midwife. "I believe you, Monsieur Fargo, *mais oui*. But the men . . ."

He cast a nervous glance around. His men, also armed, seemed on the verge of panic.

"Twice," he resumed, "we have seen the *peaux-rouges* watching us. The men would feel safer on the river."

Rip's lips curled into a sneer as he watched the wide-eyed Creoles. "The sniveling pups," he muttered to Fargo. "You said it's rough in New Orleans."

"Plenty rough, but wild Indians are new to them, and they all grew up hearing tales of scalping and torture."

"It is not just childish fear," Etienne insisted. "A boat anchored here earlier. The captain of voyageurs swears there is an Indian uprising throughout this area. He heard that we will be scalped if we stay."

"He *heard*, huh? You can't believe all you hear, but you can sure's hell repeat it," Fargo said, his tone heavy with sarcasm. "Look, Etienne, do you trust me?"

"*Mais oui*, Monsieur Fargo. You are a great frontiersman."

"All right, then listen. There's *no* Indian uprising. It's true there's a small band of renegade Comanches in these parts, but you have too many men with guns, and they won't attack. Indians place a high value on their lives, and won't risk death just to plunder."

Etienne nodded, not looking quite convinced.

"Far as whatever Indians are watching you," Fargo continued patiently, "no need to get snow in your boots. Indians always watch outsiders traveling through their territory. Just keep your men sober and post guards after dark."

"You are riding out again?"

Fargo nodded. "We have to. That boat you said stopped here earlier—it's headed right for a trap about two hours upriver. And I'll guarandamntee it's white men springing the trap, not Indians. You can't sail this boat again, Etienne, until these river pirates are wiped out."

By now Etienne looked more convinced. A steely resolve came into his eyes. "Once a man mates with despair, he is worthless."

"H'ar now," Rip approved. "Now you're whistling."

Etienne said, "Monsieur Majors told me that you are to be obeyed in all matters of security, Monsieur Fargo. I will gather the men and tell them: here we are safe. On the river, we will die."

Heading west again, Fargo forded the river and put the Ovaro to a swift gait, hammering the stallion's ribs with his boot heels.

Rip's little Indian scrub, fully recovered from being penned up on the river, gamely kept pace.

Fargo knew it was sure death to ride the river, so they veered up onto the bluffs at the lip of the valley. Before too long they overtook the keelboat, visible down below them and heading like a lamb to slaughter—or so Fargo assumed, for he had no proof river pirates were waiting to strike.

They covered more ground, Fargo occasionally sneaking to the edge of the bluff to get his bearings.

"Rip!" he called out from behind a scrub oak. "Dismount and come here."

When the old ranger had joined him, Fargo pointed to a cottonwood, with a lightning-scarred trunk, on the Indian side of the Red River.

"Recognize it?"

"Sure. That's the spot where them Winslowe twins was wadin' in the river. And there's the other tree right across from it on the Texas side."

Since the sun was behind him, Fargo broke out his field glasses and studied the nearest tree.

"See a rope?" Rip asked, his voice tight with anticipation.

"Sure as sun in the morning." Fargo replied. "And plenty more, too. Take the glasses and look about fifty yards back from the Texas bank."

"Shit, piss, and corruption," Rip muttered, almost whispering. "Here's the elephant, Fargo."

Fargo didn't need field glasses to spot the men—nine or ten of them—holed up in a little gully studded with rocks. Clearly they meant to surge forward once the keelboat was snagged.

"Look at them murderin' bastards grin," Rip said. "They figure this is gonna be easy meat."

"They've all dismounted and hobbled their horses," Fargo said, "except for Bradford."

"Ahuh, I see him settin' a white-faced bay. That smirkin' bastard would steal the coppers from a dead man's eyes, then rape his widow. I see Clint and Stone, too, but no Bo—you musta stove him up bad, Fargo."

"Breaks my damn heart. How many hired thugs do you count, Rip? I saw six."

"Ahuh. Six. Wait now. . . . Here, take a gander under them

shade trees left of the gully—ain't that Justin Halfpenny, the blacksmith?"

Fargo took the glasses back. Justin was indeed waiting in a large freight wagon hitched to four big dray horses. But his face was a mask of misery, and he was not associating with the others.

"Yeah, it's Halfpenny. I got a hunch," Fargo surmised aloud, "that he's been roped into this. Just like Belinda's been roped into being Stone's 'wife.'"

"Ahuh. A blacksmith would be useful to men stealing freight. It's easy for them big wagons to bust an iron tire."

Fargo swung the glasses back onto Bradford. Even from here Fargo could see the malice gleaming in his fierce, dark eyes. There was an air of brooding discontent about him that Fargo had learned to respect in an opponent.

"Well, Mr. Philadelphia lawyer," Rip said, "you finally got all the *proof* you need?"

"Proof, yes. Information, no. There's more to this than meets the eye. But at least we know what this bunch is, and all bets are off now. From here on out, we'll just cold-deck the bastards."

"Listen to this jay! There's too many agin us, Fargo, and no help to be had."

"For a Texas Ranger," Fargo scoffed, "you give up too easy."

"Happens we'da borrowed a half dozen of them Cherokees—"

"We've already skinned that grizz," Fargo cut him off. "This can be done by wit and wile."

"For starters, how will wit and wile keep that rope from stoppin' the keelboat?"

Fargo glanced down the steep face of the bluff. "A man's got to match his gait to the horse he's riding. Which means I'll have to sneak down there and cut the rope on our side."

"You plan to *what*?"

"I don't believe I stuttered," Fargo said calmly. "My buckskins blend in with sand, and there's a few bushes for cover. Plus there's runoff seams I can hide in."

"Ahuh. Well, man proposes, but God disposes."

"I don't know God personally," Fargo said. "But I don't think He's on *their* side in this fight. Look, bawl-baby, there's no way to wangle out of it. If that boat gets snagged, do *you* want to sit up here and watch the entire crew get slaughtered?"

Rip heaved a sigh of nervous resignation. "Ahh, you're right, lad, even though the dumb bastards tried to shoot us. But take care—they's plenty of killers just across that river."

"Hell's legion," Fargo agreed. "Make sure you keep our horses back out of sight."

He raised the glasses for one last look. Bradford had ridden to a nearby knoll to serve as lookout. Still mounted, he shifted his gun belt, threw a leg around the horn, and built himself a cigarette.

Watching him, Fargo felt his nape tingle. He knew he was not up against men—these were reptilian killing machines, especially the Winslowe brothers.

Fargo removed his gun belt, keeping only his Arkansas toothpick. "Don't wait supper for me," he joked, rolling quickly over the lip of the bluff.

Fargo had survived a dangerous life by perfecting many skills, one of them cover and concealment. Staying beneath ground level was critical now as he scrabbled downward, and when he couldn't he moved quick as a striking snake to minimize exposure. When possible he kept a hawthorn bush or a stunted jack pine between himself and the outlaws.

Soon his elbows and knees were scraped raw, but so far no gunshots had rung out. He made it to the cottonwood tree undetected. Cutting the rope was the easy part, but now came the real danger—it took only moments for the fast, spring-swollen current of the Red River to pull the loose end of the rope into the river. Stone weights took it under, but how long would it take one of those jackals on the Texas side to notice it was missing?

But Fargo caught a break when Bradford, still on the lookout, shouted, "Here she comes, boys!"

This diverted everyone's attention downriver. However, as he turned to retrace his path upward, Fargo got a bad jolt: a clump of brush in the middle of that rock-strewn gully was suddenly flattened when two men rolled a cannon forward.

"Pile on the agony," he muttered as he clawed his way up the bluff.

"Yeah, I seen it," Rip greeted him at the top. "How do we play this?"

"Remember, that cannon is for *sinking* the boat when they're done with it. They expect that boat to snag on the rope. Then they plan to kill everybody, offload supplies, and burn the keelboat. They can't plan to use that cannon first, or they'd sink the boat too soon."

"Ahuh, but you cut the rope, and now that boat will glide right past. Won't they use the cannon to stop it? Wet freight is better than none."

Fargo nodded. "Right as rain. So the main mile is to make sure nobody fires it. Take these."

He handed Rip his Colt and spare cylinder. "Your dragoon holds five loads. I'll fire my Henry. That gives each of us plenty of rounds to make it hot for them."

"We'll have to expose ourselves to get a plumb bead," Rip fretted. "With all them guns down there, it's gonna be one hell of a shooting bee."

"I won't paint the lily," Fargo said. "It'll be a rough piece of work. Those hired jobbers are just your run-of-the-range trash, and normally they'd hit the breeze at the first well-aimed shots. But the Winslowe boys will put some stiff in their spines, so *don't* waste any bullet."

"I see the sail," Rip exclaimed. "Won't be long now."

"Those greedy bastards still haven't noticed the cut rope," Fargo remarked, watching the river pirates through his field glasses.

Bradford rode down into the gully, hobbled his bay, then began creeping closer to the river with the others. Justin was busy hooking the tug chains to the harness.

"Clint's got that modified Spencer," Fargo said, his face grim. "I'll have a better chance at him, since this is rifle range, so he'll be my first target. You've got short guns, so concentrate on the men closest to the river."

Fargo stepped back to the Ovaro, snatched the Henry from its scabbard, and jacked a round into the chamber. The sights were set for game, about two hundred yards, and he left them alone.

The keelboat was clearly visible on the river below.

"Now?" Rip demanded.

"Just hold your powder," Fargo ordered. "Let it get closer."

"Stone!" one of the men shouted a minute later, pointing toward the cottonwood. "The motherlovin' rope came loose!"

"Now we'll see how these killers like turnabout," Fargo muttered. "Open fire!"

Fargo didn't forget his vow—he dropped the notch sight on Clint Winslowe's chest, squeezed off a round, and saw a gout of blood spurt from the outlaw's chest before he folded to the ground dead, landing atop that lethal rifle.

"Up on the bluff!" Stone roared, and moments later a wall of lead hurtled in on them. But both men lay in place, shell casings glinting in the sunlight as they maintained their fire.

Fargo saw a thin, hard-knit, rawboned man leap into action, ramming powder into the cannon. Fargo's first shot missed, but he levered the Henry, adjusted his aim, and his next shot punched into the man's neck.

By now the keelboat was nearly alongside, and Stone, who had ducked for cover, looked frantic.

"Don't stand there gawking, moon-calves!" he roared out. "You, Skotinski—*fire* that damn thing before the boat gets by!"

A man with thinning red hair and a hard little face like a terrier leaped to the cannon. However, by now the boat crew was returning fire, and Fargo saw the face of the hired thug melt in a spray of buckshot.

That third death broke the back of the attack. Besieged from bluffs and river, with several men wounded, Stone called a retreat. The desperadoes fled south into Texas while the keelboat glided safely west.

"We *done* it!" Rip shouted, standing up when Fargo did. "By Godfrey, we done it!"

Fargo, however, had made one mistake—he'd lost track of Bradford Winslowe. A glint of light on the far bank caught his eye only a heartbeat before a gun muzzle spat orange flame. A mule kick to Fargo's rib cage was followed by a burst of fiery pain, and the Trailsman crumpled to the ground.

10

"Is it mortal, Fargo?" Rip asked for perhaps the third time, repeating himself in his anxiety for his friend.

Fargo, wincing with pain, pulled off his buckskin shirt. Angry red flesh had puckered the entry wound on his left rib cage. "It's more than a graze—he definitely plugged me in the side."

"Can you taste blood?"

Fargo shook his head.

Rip grinned. "That means it missed your lung. And there's another hole in your back muscle—that bullet sailed clean through you. Ain't hardly no blood, neither, on account it mostly tore through muscle, which you got plenty of. You're lucky, boy, but a muscle wound *will* smart—worse tomorrow than it does today."

"I've had worse, Rip. Jesus, he got that close to my lights with a *handgun* at two hundred yards. That son of a bitch is death to the devil. I know he recognized us. We better play this mighty smart from now on, or he'll point our toes to the sky. Is that him I hear riding south?"

Rip crept cautiously to the edge of the bluff. "Ahuh. He's catching up with the rest, prob'ly braggin' how he done for you. Say—they left that cannon behind."

"They'll be back for it," Fargo said, his words punctuated with hissing sips of pain. "And Stone won't leave Clint's body, either."

He hooked a thumb toward his Ovaro. "You'll find a bottle of carbolic and a bandage roll in the nearside saddle pocket. Fetch 'em, wouldja?"

Rip carefully poured carbolic acid in the entrance wound.

"You did a good job on that bluff," Fargo praised him.

"Why, tarnal hell! I don't think I hit one man."

"With a short gun? At this distance, who, besides Bradford

Winslowe and a circus trick shooter, could? I have trouble hitting beyond thirty yards with my Colt. The thing of it is, you tossed plenty of lead in among them, rattling and unnerving them. And not once did you shirk back, even with rounds pluming in all around you nineteen to the dozen. You *are* just the right boy when the war whoop sounds."

"Ahh, no need to slop over," Rip said, obviously pleased.

"This doesn't mean we're swapping spit," Fargo hastened to add. "You're still a stinking old relic who gets drunk on guard duty."

"Happens you want doctorin', you best shut pan. Roll onto your other side so's I can get at that exit wound."

"Damn and double damn," Fargo cursed when he did as ordered. "That hurts like hell. Say, you got any more of those jokes of yours?"

"So you *do* like 'em?"

"Hell no. But when I have a toothache, stubbing my toe takes my mind off it."

"Fargo, you're as funny as a smallpox blanket. Anyhow, these two Kansas City whores was workin' the topside of a saloon. One says to the other, 'Rosie, do you smoke after a man screws you?' And Rosie says, 'I don't know—I never looked.'"

Fargo groaned. "Jesus, I'll stick with the wound."

"Speakin' of that," Rip said, "here's somethin' that *ain't* so funny. This exit wound looks too big to just flush out and cover— I'm thinkin' it might putrify if it ain't cauterized."

"I was afraid of that," Fargo said. "Use my knife. You'll find crumbled bark and kindling in my saddle pockets, but be quick about it, Rip. That gang got shot up pretty bad, but the Winslowes lost a brother, and they could double back anytime."

Rip built a small fire and kept it burning just long enough to heat the blade of the Arkansas toothpick until it glowed blood orange. Then, giving Fargo no warning it was coming, he laid the red-hot steel over the exit wound. Fargo went rigid with indescribable pain, loosing every curse word known to man and adding a few to the lexicon.

A crackling, sizzling noise was followed by the stench of scorched meat. The moment the hole had sealed itself, Rip bathed it in water from his canteen.

"There," he announced, sleeving sweat off his brow, "it's did."

"If I don't get a poultice on that soon," Fargo said weakly, "the pain will get worse than dying."

"Ahuh. We need a camp where you can lay up for a day or so. Got any big ideas?"

Grimacing, Fargo sat up. "These Winslowes and their hired curs—they ain't plainsmen. They're murderers and thieves, not men who know how to survive in the open spaces. They're not trackers, either. I say we ride north again, find a good campsite."

"I'll grant all that. But Comanches are damn good plainsmen."

"Top-notch," Fargo agreed. "But tell me—you've fought Comanches. Once they decide to kill a man, do they pussyfoot around about it?"

"Hell no. They come right at their enemy like the devil beating bark."

"You better know they do. Well, we took a long ride north yesterday, and a long ride back today. And we've been up and down this valley in plain sight."

"Ahuh." Rip mulled it. "Think they gave up on us?"

Fargo struggled to stand, and Rip helped him up. "Maybe. Or more likely they found a better target of opportunity. A way station, a detail of soldiers, who knows? One thing for sure, after this shooting fray today we can't camp in the valley."

Rip pointed across the river. "So we just leave that cannon? They'll be back for it."

Face twisting with fiery pain, Fargo stepped into a stirrup and gingerly pushed up and over. "Sure they will, but what choice we got? We don't have the tools to spike the barrel, and if we push it into the river it could sink a keelboat. Besides, I'm in no shape for hard labor."

Both men gigged their horses north.

"You heard the one about Lu-lu girl and the drunk preacher?" Rip said, and Fargo begged for mercy.

"Boys, the cannon is hid again," Stone Winslowe reported to his brothers. "And the men I got out riding report no sign of that lanky son of a bitch. But that don't cut no ice with me. I say he's just laying low."

"He's 'laying low,' all right," Bradford boasted, "on account I killed him. That old man took the body and buried it so we wouldn't know."

"How can you know that?" Bo demanded. His face was still swollen from the beating "that lanky son of a bitch" gave him, and his lips still so puffy they slurred his speech.

"Because I saw him drop," Bradford retorted. "Like a sack of potatoes. And we ain't seen any sign of him since, have we?"

"But did you drill his vitals?" Bo pressured. "You're a dead aim, all right, but that was rifle range. Do you know, for a *fact*, you plugged his lights?"

"Christ, how could I, brother? I wasn't up on that bluff."

Stone, sitting on the plank counter, pulled a thin Mexican cigar from his vest, then thumb-snapped a lucifer to life and leaned into the flame. "Bradford admits he can't know that—the distance was too great. So that bastard ain't dead until we see the body."

Belinda, whom Stone seldom let out of his sight for very long, sat behind the men, filling several coal-oil lamps and trimming the wicks. She tried to look unconcerned, but this talk about Fargo's death made her hands tremble—if *he* was dead, so, too, was any hope of surviving this living nightmare.

Bradford, his back propped against the north wall, gave a contemptuous laugh. "Katy Christ! A bunch of damn women fret like this, not men who own a pair."

"You weren't close by the rest of us," Stone reminded his arrogant brother, "when Dutch Phil recognized Fargo. Dutch Phil was running a sutler store at Fort Sill when Fargo was hired as chief of scouts. He says the man is at the top of the heap. He can track, shoot, and use his fists like no man he ever saw. Plus, he's tricky as a redheaded woman, and I reckon we know *that*. I thought about it the whole time we was burying Clint."

"All that," Bradford scoffed, "is what they call 'bubbling hearsay.' Dutch Phil, my ampersand! That drunken sot don't know his ass from his elbow. Say, I'll bet this 'Trailsman' can light a match with a whip, too, hey? And maybe ride cyclones?"

Bo doubled his fists. "He killed Clint—ain't that enough? And look at my face."

"You boys are building a pimple into a peak," Bradford insisted. "Far as Clint, he died like a man, and I'm proud of him. As for Fargo, he's either already gone up the flume or soon will. *I'll* see to that."

"Don't piss down our backs and tell us it's raining!" Bo exploded. "First you swore you killed him—now he *might* be dead."

77

Bradford pushed away from the wall, gunmetal eyes watching Bo. He fingered the heavy brass studding of his gun belt as if it were piano keys. "If you're feeling froggy, little brother, go ahead and jump."

"No, thanks. I'm quick, but you're quicker than eyesight."

"Damn straight I am, and ten men, so far, have found that out. So if Fargo ain't dead, he can just get set to cash in."

"What the hell is this?" Stone demanded. "Bradford, are you threatening to kill your own brother after he just buried his twin?"

"Ahh, you know I'm just running a bluff, Stone."

"Uh-huh. Well, everything, to you, is a draw-shoot contest. But gun throwers ain't the only killers. Why should Fargo face off with you if he can pop you over at rifle range or toss that Arkansas toothpick into your back?"

Bradford grinned. "Because he's a proud man with a 'code.' And I forced his hand the first day we saw him. He won't abide those insults, and we'll be locking horns, all right. He's cold meat, I'm telling you."

Despite Bradford's harsh boasts, Belinda noticed, she could clearly see the worry lines starched into the other two men's faces, and seeing it thrilled her. Until this tall man in buckskins came along, "fear" was not in their vocabulary. But *was* he still alive?

"I believe you can gun him down," Stone conceded, "but if you don't do it in a puffin' hurry, we're ruint. That keelboat— the whole damn shebang sailed right on by us, and it's all that meddling bastard's fault. Do you boys realize how much money that son of a bitch Fargo cost us? I already had a buyer in Santa Fe."

"You said Fargo worked for the army," Bo chimed in. "Could be he's got officer friends. Maybe we should all clear out before the army twigs our game."

Stone snorted. "The hell's got into you—religion?"

"We only paid for a license to trade," Bo reminded him. "Not to rob teamsters and keelboats."

"Stone's right," Bradford said. "This is no time to go puny. On the frontier, ain't nothing cheaper than a man's life—we're staying here."

"Damn straight we are," Stone asserted. "Caswell Jones is due any day now, and we ain't got enough to make a full load. But—"

He broke off suddenly when he noticed Belinda listening attentively. "You bolted to that stool, woman? Go back and get some coffee boiling."

"Yes, Stone," she said submissively, rising immediately and heading toward the door to the living quarters. But she heard some of his remark before she reached the door.

". . . but that keelboat is still anchored downriver, and they'll have to set sail sooner or later."

Fargo waited patiently in the copse of trees near the river, hoping Belinda would decide to use her private bathing pool. This time, however, he had come heeled, and the Ovaro was hobbled in sandbar willows near the river just west of the trading post. He knew this play was dicey, and twice he spotted outriders on his way here, but he figured his enemies wouldn't be looking for him in their very midst.

The day stretched into late morning, then early afternoon, the sun heating up. Fargo was about to give it up as a bad job when the wooden gate in the wall creaked open. He watched Belinda, her curls a luminous gold in the sunlight, glide down the path toward him. Her pretty, fine-boned face was a careful blank slate, and Fargo admired the way a thin blue cotton dress traced her stunning body as if she were naked.

"Skye?" she called out in a low, hopeful tone before she had even spotted him. "I couldn't risk coming sooner. Are you here?"

"Been here a long time, darlin', and the wait was worth it."

"Oh! You *are* alive!"

The moment the trees screened her from the trading post she flew to him, pressing warm, soft curves tightly against him. "Bradford bragged that he killed you."

Fargo hissed with pain when she embraced him, irritating the wound on his left side. "Easy there, girl. He almost did. Take a peek at his handiwork."

He pulled his buckskin shirt up to show her the angry red flesh. "It's still a mite stiff, but it's a long way from my heart."

"That *pig*! I hope you kill him twice."

Fargo chuckled. "Once is usually sufficient."

"Speaking of once being enough . . . we need to talk, but Stone is jittery and might come outside at any moment. So I was hoping we might take care of something first, and I took some liberties . . ."

She grabbed the skirt of her dress and tugged the garment off. No petticoats, no chemise, no pantaloons: just lotion-smooth, naked flesh pale as moonstone.

"Am I a wanton?" she asked coyly, watching Fargo feast his eyes on full, hard, high breasts, voluptuous hips, and a dark blond triangle of hair that grew to a point where her split began.

Suddenly Fargo was stiff in two places. He dropped his gun belt, then swept her off her feet and laid her down in the deep grass and sweet clover, taking one of her spearmint-tasting nipples into his mouth as he fumbled open his fly. He licked and nibbled until both nipples were hard and she was whimpering with pleasure and hunger.

"*Do* me, Skye!" she begged in a breathless voice. "Oh, put that magnificent man gland deep inside me."

There were times when Fargo loved being ordered around, and this was one of them. Her thighs, when he parted them wide, were smooth and silky to the touch. His blood pounding with lust, he opened the chamois folds of her nether portal to make room. Then he trust deep into her velvet heat, feeling the walls of her sex expanding to accommodate him.

"Take me, Skye, take me hard! I just want to forget."

Her hot talk already had Fargo het up, and he drove into her fast and powerfully, coaxing little surprised cries and incoherent words from her each time she peaked. Fargo felt his own release was imminent and cupped his hands under her taut buttocks, pulling her even closer as he spent himself in shuddering release.

When her daze finally passed and thought returned, Belinda sighed. "They say the Lord busted the mold after he made the Trailsman. Now I see why."

"Maybe He just didn't like what He made."

"Well, I sure do."

Fargo realized what she'd just said. "Hold on—where did you ever hear me called the Trailsman?"

"One of the men you fought, day before yesterday, recognized you and told the Winslowe brothers all about you." She flashed pretty white teeth at him. "Including about what a womanizer you are. I'm glad it's my turn."

Fargo buckled on his gun belt. "So they prob'ly told you about that scrape at the river?"

"They don't actually *tell* me anything, but I overhear plenty.

You see, I'm allowed out of Stone's sight only to bathe or . . . stretch my legs," she said, a lady's euphemism meaning to answer the call of nature. "He doesn't really need to watch me close because he knows I dare not run away. He's just afraid some other man will . . ."

Fargo grinned and finished her point. "Do what I just did with you. Belinda, how are the Winslowe brothers acting since that fight at the river?"

"Oh, you've got them nerve-frazzled, Skye, but also mad-dog mean. Clint is dead, Bo looks like a stampede went over his face, and Stone is losing money. The only one who's still cool as a cucumber is Bradford. Nothing scares him much. He's got no more fear in him than a rifle."

"He's trouble," Fargo agreed. "Five men like Bradford could take over England. I was hoping he believed he killed me."

"He brags that he did, but even he's not sure."

Fargo explained the freight-stealing operation, so far as he understood it, and Belinda filled in the important missing link.

"Part of their ring is a crooked boatman named Caswell Jones and his crew. He has a huge keelboat, twice the size of most. The trading post shelves are nearly empty now because the brothers have put together a shipment for Jones to take into west Texas, where the river shrinks to a trickle stream. From there it's hauled overland to Santa Fe and sold to caravan outfitters. It's a large operation started by Stone."

"So he's the head of the snake?"

She nodded. "And Stone is dangerous, Skye. But never forget, it's Bradford you must fear most. You must think I mention him too often, but I've seen him kill, and his draw is so fast you miss it if you blink. He's one of these new breed of 'draw-shoot' killers you read about in *Police Gazette*."

Fargo nodded. "Not just fast, right? Deadly accurate, too?"

"Terrifyingly accurate. He can put six bullets in a target and leave only one hole, like Robin Hood splitting his own arrow."

Fargo gingerly touched his wound. "I've experienced his accuracy firsthand. Most handgun shooters couldn't hit a man at one-third of the distance he covered to hit me."

"I can tell from the way he talks and the look in your eyes—it's coming down to you and him, isn't it?"

"Looks that way," Fargo conceded.

"Well, my money is on you. Oh, one more thing—Stone has to make up for the cargo you cost him, and he's mentioned another keelboat that's anchored downriver."

"I figured that. Help me out with something else," Fargo told her. "Besides Bradford, I have to whip these other two owlhoots, and I know little about them."

"Well," she said as she buttoned her dress, "Bo isn't exactly the brightest spark in the campfire—Stone claims he was mule-kicked in the head as a child. But he's tough, and stubborn, and he can handle guns. As for Stone . . ."

Fargo saw a shudder move through her despite the day's heat. "Stone . . . the man's very name is gall and wormwood to me! He is cunning, and strong like all the brothers, and he has the most ambition. He's also the sickest—sickest in the mind, I mean."

A tearful catch in her throat, as she finished her remarks, told Fargo how much strain she was under. "I would gladly cut his throat in his sleep if . . . if I could. But that's impossible."

Fargo made sure the path was still empty and the gate closed. "Look, Belinda, there's no need to be bashful with me. None of this is your fault, so tell me—is it just Stone who calls you 'wife,' or does he force his brothers on you, too?"

"No sharing at all, Skye. In fact, *no* man has had me, except you, since we—I mean, *I* was taken prisoner."

Fargo looked astounded. "A beautiful gal like you, blessed by nature?"

She nodded. "You see, Stone is a dog in the manger. He's incapable of . . . you know, taking a woman?"

"He can't get hard, you mean?"

"Exactly, although every night he tries. And he doesn't want his brothers to find that out, so he pretends to hog me—his right as the oldest brother. Since he can't have me, no man will."

Fargo grinned. "Somebody forgot to tell me that."

"Oh, my stars, are you ever *capable*."

Fargo's grin faced. "Listen, have you heard that old saying 'the best way to cure a boil is to lance it'?"

She nodded.

"Well, starting tonight there's going to be some . . . violence around here. You need to vamoose while I can still take you. Will you leave with me now?"

She shook her head stubbornly. "I can't. I already told you that."

"Yeah, and I'm getting tired of playing button-button-who's-got-the-button. The reason you won't leave is because Stone and his brothers are holding loved ones of yours, right?"

"Skye, I'm sorry, but—"

"I figure you, your husband, and maybe a kid or two set out on the Oregon Trail. Some grifter in St. Joe or Independence sold you a phony map showing a southern 'shortcut' that avoids South Pass and the mountains. You ended up out here, lost, and the Winslowes nabbed you. I've seen it dozens of times."

Her pretty face flushed with indignation. "Skye Fargo, you are the world-beatingest man! Such conceit! My husband? Yes, you're handsome, but if I were married, do you think I'd be wallowing in the grass with you like some shameless tart?"

Plenty of married women already had, but Fargo discreetly let that point die. "All right, then, your ma and pa, maybe some other kin?"

She sat silent for at least ten seconds, a tear quivering on her right eyelid. "Now you've got it right," she finally said. "My mother, father, and little brother, Scotty. Pa bought the phony map in St. Joe, all right."

"So that's the way of it," Fargo said. "And what about Justin Halfpenny?"

"He's a good man, Skye, though naive like Pa. He left the wagon train to travel with us. They're holding his wife with my family."

"Where?"

She shook her head adamantly. "This is where I draw the line, Skye. Escape is impossible so long as one Winslowe is still alive. Once those monsters are killed, you'll be the first to know where my people are. Justin won't talk either, I assure you."

"All right, lady. They've put you through hell, and it's your call. But with or without your cooperation, I aim to get all of you free. I can't promise to do it, but I promise to try even if it kills me."

11

The night was black as new tar—perfect for the work Fargo had in mind. He and Rip hobbled their horses in the same sandbar willows Fargo had used earlier that day, a good vantage point just past the trading post compound.

"These trips into town are risky, Fargo," Rip complained as both men blackened their faces with gunpowder from Rip's horn.

"And they'll be even riskier after this little fandango tonight. So what? What's the good of dodging the fare if we lose our freight?"

"What freight? The hell you talkin' about?"

"It's a manner of speaking," Fargo replied impatiently. "Look, a Texas Ranger ought to know about risks."

"I got no dicker with taking risks," Rip objected, "happens they stand a snowball's chance. You really think this will work?"

"Not by itself, but it's a start—especially after that shootout at the river day before yesterday. Remember, old son, this ain't a town with solid citizens. It's not even a crossroads settlement. Hell, it's a bull-and-bear pit. These are murdering and thieving cowards, and they're not about to die just so the Winslowes can get rich."

Rip grunted assent as they moved cautiously out of the trees. "Hell, all that shines. How many killings has this God-forgotten hellhole already notched?"

"That's the gait," Fargo approved. "First we scrape away the maggots, and that exposes the flies—all three of them. Got your torch?"

"Ahuh. Don't see why we need torches, though. They make us better targets. A lucifer will get 'er done."

"Think so, huh?" Fargo halted Rip with a hand on his shoulder. "Just listen."

84

After only ten seconds or so, a harsh north wind howled with a sound like souls in torment and pressed the grass flat.

"Using just a lucifer, in these gusts," Fargo pointed out, "will force us to get too close or it'll blow out. When you're ready, just fire up the torch and throw it. Then bust out of here like a hound with his ass afire."

Fargo lowered his voice as they slipped past the dark trading post, sticking close to the riverbank. Despite his assurances to Rip, Fargo harbored no illusions about the hardcases in this mud-and-canvas camp: they were men unfamiliar with opera houses and good grooming, but well versed in cold-blooded murder.

Cat-footed, they moved up from the murmuring river into the wretched wallow that served as the only street. Now the clamor of drunken revelry almost drowned out the wind gusts. Oily yellow light poured from the two canvas saloons, illuminating a couple dozen mounts with their bridles down. Fargo groped in one of the many trash heaps until he found two unbroken bottles.

"Cover me," he whispered. "If I get caught filling these two bottles, spray some lead and then hotfoot it back to the horses."

Fargo's observant eye and nose had noticed, when he first rode into this roach pit, what smelled like a community vat of coal oil setting on a fat stump beside the Bucket of Blood. It was probably provided by Stone Winslowe as part of the effort to facilitate nighttime drinking and keep these owlhoots from drifting on.

Fargo shoved the torch behind his gun belt. Then he moved in quickly and worked the crude wooden spigot, filling both bottles.

He was almost finished when a drunk staggered outside and jerked his pistol. Howling like a mad wolf, he unleashed three shots at the night sky. Fargo tensed, fearing Rip would open fire, but the old-timer held his powder.

"Kiss my ass, old man moon, wherever the hell you are!" he brayed.

The drunk reeled inside again, and Fargo joined his friend, handing him a bottle.

"I almost powder-burned that yahoo," Rip said.

"Good thing you didn't. Now listen—as soon as you get behind the Sawdust Corner, soak the canvas with coal oil. The minute you see mine flare up, light your torch and toss it on the canvas. Then run like hell toward the sandbar. Don't bother to cover your retreat—just hoof it out of there."

"Don't cover my—hell, Fargo, these ain't Quakers. Somebody's liable to come after me."

"So what? They're all so drunk they're walking on their knees, and it's pitch-black out here. Their eyes are adjusted to the light inside the tents. Besides, they'll all come after me—I'm going to make sure of it. That's why I brought the Henry."

The two men parted and went behind their respective saloons. The din inside the Bucket of Blood told Fargo most of these men were staggering drunk. He splashed coal oil onto his dead-grass torch, then all over the canvas.

Fargo snapped a lucifer into flame, ignited the torch, then shouted in a voice powerful enough to fill a canyon: "Clear out or *die*, you lily-livered mange pots!"

He tossed his torch just as a powerful gust of wind kicked up, and the entire structure seemed to burst into flame at once. Suddenly the party inside was over as screaming, cursing, shocked-silent men poured outside, each clawing and kicking to be first.

Almost simultaneously, the Sawdust Corner exploded in flames, and the chaotic scene was repeated on the other side of the wallow. Fargo, deliberately diverting the attention to himself, opened up with the Henry, buying time for the older, slower Rip to escape. He reluctantly avoided hitting anyone, even in this gathering of jackals, deeming it murder.

At first the panicked and confused drunks had no idea where the shots were coming from. Then, in the flickering firelight, a doltish-looking, slope-shouldered man saw Fargo and raised the hue and cry. A quick snap shot from the Henry punched a slug into his thigh, and the man's warning words got lost in his howls of pain.

Figuring Rip had a good head start, Fargo began his scoot-and-shoot retreat, running several yards and spinning around to fire, keeping the local denizens ducking. But another man had spotted him and chased recklessly after him, short gun blazing. Fargo whirled, dropped to one knee, levered the Henry, and squeezed off a round, plugging his would-be assassin in the eye. His hideous shrieks of pain had the effect of a Comanche war cry, stopping the rest in their tracks. A few, however, still fired blind into the darkness.

"Fargo! I'm right here," Rip's voice said in the darkness ahead. "You all right, old codger?"

"Spry and chipper as ever. Hell, you got them peckerwoods all flummoxed. Let me toss a few Kentucky pills at 'em, too."

Fargo grabbed Rip's arm. "Never mind. We'd just be shooting at shadows. Best to conserve our ammo—we'll be needing it before this is over. Besides, the muzzle flash from that big dragoon will give them a target. Let's hit leather and light a shuck out of here."

It looked like a clean getaway lay ahead. But as Fargo and Rip trotted past the rear of the trading post, the wooden gate was suddenly flung open. Despite the fact that both men were swallowed up by a moonless night, a shooter opened up on them with impressive accuracy—six shots that hornet-buzzed past their ears.

"Kiss the grass," Fargo whispered.

Both men went flat on the riverbank.

"God's gumbo," Rip muttered. "Whoever that is must have the eyes of a cat."

"Take a guess who it is," Fargo retorted.

His trail-honed ears heard a spare cylinder being snapped into place. Six more shots rang out, several parting the deep grass near their heads. When yet another cylinder snapped into place, Fargo cursed and threw the Henry into his shoulder.

At the next orange streak from the gate, Fargo unloaded several shots as fast as he could jack the bullets into the chamber, rolling immediately to a new position.

"Go!" he ordered Rip, snapping off three more shots to force the marksman to cover down while they ran the last fifty yards to the sandbar willows.

Fargo's strategy worked. No more shots sounded from the gate. But the unmistakable sound of Bradford Winslowe's cocky, arrogant voice chased them into the trees like a wolverine snapping at their heels:

"I'm the Grim Reaper, Fargo, and you're my favorite boy! The death hug's coming real soon, hear me? *Real* goddamn soon!"

Once within the willows, Fargo sheathed his still-warm Henry. Then he cinched the saddle girth tight, removed the Ovaro's rawhide hobbles, and vaulted into the saddle, shaking out the reins.

"Let's get this medicine show on the road, Methuselah," he urged Rip. "Drunks are real fond of getting up posses. You should've used hobbles, not a picket line."

"Lost 'em somewhere, *sonny*," the old-timer shot back, finally pulling out his picket pin.

Grunting at the effort, Rip stepped up into leather and immediately fell on his ass, cussing like a bullwhacker on a muddy road, when the loose saddle slid around.

"You old fool," Fargo berated him. "You know the rule: when you leave your horse with the girth loose, you put a stirrup on the saddle horn to remind you."

"I did, consarn it! I didn't see it in the dark, is all. Ain't no green on *my* antlers."

Rip finally got squared away and the two men rode hard to the west, then looped back to the east, swinging wide of the trading post. Once clear of that, they stayed close to the river and held their mounts to an easy lope.

After Bradford had wounded Fargo, two days earlier, Rip and the Trailsman had made a cold camp on the plains north of the river. Rip had insisted, however, that his old cave up in the bluffs was more secure. Leery of holing up so close to the river, Fargo had nonetheless agreed to look at it.

After only a quick inspection, Fargo had agreed with the old salt. The cave entrance, obscured by a sandstone tumble, allowed a partial view of the river but did not emit light, permitting fires within. A rear chamber was large enough to hold both horses and included a small seep spring where they could drink at will. It also held a welcome supply of jerked buffalo.

After their successful escape from the outlaw haven, both men led their horses for the last half mile to cool them out. Once inside the cave, Fargo built a driftwood fire inside a circle of rocks. Then he and Rip stripped the leather from their mounts and rubbed them down with old gunnysacks.

"Fargo," Rip speculated aloud, "I take your drift, and I'm thinkin' maybe you *can* drive Stone's lickspittles out of The Nations. But it ain't just Bradford—how 'bout Stone hisself? He'll live up to his name, and have you ever seen a *stone* melt?"

Fargo filled his hat with parched corn and held it for the Ovaro. "I don't want him to hightail it, Rip. He'll just start his operation somewhere else. He's the one who spread his brag about how he's the lord and master in these parts. All right, so he's the one who's going to pay for every killing."

"Hell, that shines. Matter fact, why in the name of Lot's wife *should* they leave? Ain't no law in these parts to stop them from what they're doin'."

"Oh, there's 'law.' Three of them tasted it two days ago, and a couple more tonight. But the killing's far from over."

Careful of his mending side, Fargo pulled the Henry from its sheath and sat near the fire to run a bore brush through the muzzle. Rip sat opposite him, trying to gnaw the tough jerky with his few remaining teeth.

"Hey, Fargo?"

The Trailsman glanced up and saw the old-timer watching him, lips twisted into a sly smile. "What?"

"I seen the grass stains on your knees when you come back earlier."

"Yeah? So what?"

"Little bit of the old slap and tickle, huh?"

"Wipe that soft-brained grin off your pan," Fargo snapped. "It's none of your beeswax."

"No need to have a conniption fit. Say, did she give you any inside skinny?"

"According to Belinda," Fargo replied, "the Winslowe brothers are rattled, all right, except for Bradford. But we don't have them on the ragged edge yet. So this is no time to let up."

Fargo also told Rip about Caswell Jones and the fact that the brothers had their eye on the anchored keelboat.

"You think them greedy bastards will attack it?" Rip asked. "While she's anchored, I mean."

Fargo shook his head. "He'll have to get more desperate first. It's easier for them to snag the boats in the river and leave the crew like sitting ducks. Freight wagons, sure, they have only two or three men to deal with. But Etienne and his voyageurs are well armed with repeating rifles, and they can take up good positions on land. Stone has lost some gunmen by now, too. But we'll keep an eye on them in case I'm wrong."

"Anyhow," Rip said, "I'm glad them bastards seen who we was up on that bluff. All your 'preacher' and 'Indian school' tomfoolery mighta got us killed. The pitcher can go back to the well once too often."

"I agree. But don't worry, they'll crater," Fargo predicted confidently. "I've flushed rats out of other holes like this. Kill one rodent, kill a million."

It was late, so as soon as he'd finished cleaning his rifle, Fargo rolled up in his blanket. Rip, however, spent several minutes gazing across Red River into the dark, shadowy mass of north Texas. Suddenly he chuckled.

"You know, Fargo, it's almost funny—Mexico invited Americans into Texas in the first place, thinkin' they'd quell the Injins. Ain't that a hoot? The beaners not only lost Texas, but low-crawlin' bastards like these Winslowe brothers are now spreadin' north of the Red. Decent folks ain't safe anywheres west of the Big Muddy."

"You talk of Texas all the time," Fargo's sleepy voice said. "Why'd you leave?"

"Ahh, some mix-up about just *who* was the father of a little baby girl. Anyhow, I do miss the chaparral country of south Texas. Mebbe I'll get back someday. They say cattle outfits will soon be starting up between the Nueces and the Rio Grande—a big beef bonanza—and they'll need hash-slingers—"

Rip fell silent when he heard Fargo's deep, even breathing.

"Well, raise my rent," he muttered. "The man goes out screwing and killing, burns down a saloon, then falls right to sleep peaceful as a baby at the tit. Somethin' tells me them Winslowe boys is playin' the cobra to his mongoose."

Fargo's eyelids popped open, and the first thing he saw, only six feet from his bedroll, was a triple-soled elkskin moccasin. His heart stomped against his ribs while his right hand reflexively tugged the Arkansas toothpick from his boot. He rolled hard and fast, coming up in a crouch with his arm cocked back to throw.

"If *you* kill me, Son of Light," the intruder said in halting English, "I will sit behind no brave at the council fires beyond the sun."

Fargo studied the Comanche warrior closely. A black obsidian knife protruded from a sheath on his hip, but he brandished no weapon. He wore the usual beaded buckskin leggings, doeskin breechclout, and bone breastplate. Like most Comanches, he was bowlegged from so much time on horseback.

"Look there at your famous stallion," the warrior boasted. "Still asleep on his feet. We Comanches can sneak into a white man's lodge and steal his sleeping wife without waking her up. But *you* woke up just in time to kill me."

Fargo was puzzled and suspicious, but like this brave kept all emotions out of his face. Only women, children, and weak white men showed feelings in their faces, and no Plains warrior respected any man who did so.

"Is that what you seek here?" Fargo replied. "Death?"

"I seek only what I find, and I have found the white warrior called Son of Light by the Navajos many sleeps' ride from here."

Fargo nodded. Nearby, Rip snored with a racket like a boar in rut. "It's a name I am proud to have."

"I am called Medicine Flute. He who may not be mentioned, the brave you gutted several sleeps ago, was my clan brother."

Many tribes, Fargo knew, never named the dead for fear they might answer. "And you came to avenge him?"

Medicine Flute shook his head. "There is no reason. He attacked you in your sleep, but you were the better man. You could have left his body on the ground, facedown, as buffalo hunters do to us. Instead, you made him a scaffold and pointed his eyes toward the High Holy Ones."

Fargo nodded but said nothing, watching and waiting.

"The warriors in my clan were puzzled by this," Medicine Flute said. "We wondered what manner of man this is. Could this be Son of Light, who saved many Navajo children from slavers? So we watched you. We saw your battle with the whiteskins at the river and your attack on the lodges where they drink strong water. I was sent here to see for myself, and now I know it is true."

Rip, only half asleep, called out, "Fargo? The hell's all that yammerin'? Can't a body get no sleep?"

"These white men," Medicine Flute continued, "are lower than a pig's afterbirth. We Comanches are hard killers, it is true, and show little quarter to those outside of our kind. But these white-eyes murder their own. And though we Comanches are called the Red Raiders of the Plains by white men, *this* land around us belongs to red men. The whiteskins have taken everything else, yet now they disobey their own talking papers called 'treaties' and take our spoils."

Fargo felt no sympathy for this renegade and felt neither

honored nor fooled by all his fawning over "Son of Light." He considered his complaints rank hypocrisy. His tribe came to The Nations only to raid and kill. Old Rip was right—Comanches were the terror of the southern plains and at one time had wiped out nearly all the white residents of Texas. Now they were doing the same in the western New Mexico Territory—and even the white killers who licked Stone Winslowe's boots did not torture women and children.

Yet, Fargo was in no position to speak his true mind. Only a few nights ago Comanches tried to murder him in his sleep, and if he insulted this brave, he and Rip would again be caught between two deadly enemies, never mind Fargo's supposed "fame" among Navajos—whose children Comanches often sold into slavery down in Mexico.

"I have ears for your words," he told Medicine Flute. "Speak them."

"Only this: the white thieves have too many thunder sticks, and we are too few to attack them. But with you and your cunning as our spearhead, we will do the hurt dance on them. You have only to summon us."

"How?"

"One of us is always nearby. Just fire your barking iron twice into the sky."

Fargo mulled it, but one fact decided him: if the white outlaws were killed or driven off, the keelboats and teamsters stood a better chance—the Comanches were loath to attack well-armed boat crews. Besides, Comanches couldn't pay off the army to look the other way.

"It is a worthy plan," Fargo said. "I am not sure when it will be, but I will signal."

Medicine Flute nodded. He turned to leave, but Fargo stopped him. He hooked a thumb toward Rip's bedroll. "A little sport?"

Now the brave's stoic face widened in a grin—like most tribes, the Comanches savored a practical joke. Medicine Flute crept close to the bedroll and pulled out his knife.

"Rip!" Fargo barked. "Up and on the line!"

"Huh? What the . . . ? *Jesus H. Christ!*"

With a horrific battle shriek, Medicine Flute grabbed the old man's long, greasy gray hair as if to scalp him.

"Murderin' red devils!" Rip cried out, too paralyzed by fear to even move. "Drill him, Fargo. He's liftin' my dander!"

Medicine Flute went through the motions of taking the entire scalp, but in fact only hacked off a few inches of hair hanging down in the back. Still yipping, he held it so Rip could see it.

"He's scalped me, Fargo!" the old man wailed. "I felt it poppin' like bubbles when he tore it off! You heathen son of a bitch, I'll irrigate your guts!"

Medicine Flute stole out of the cave, still grinning, while Rip groped for his dragoon pistol. "Oh, God's garters, it hurts like all git-out! Where'd he go, Fargo?"

Speaking between bursts of laughter, Fargo said, "Feel your head, you old fool."

"I ain't touchin' that bloody mess—*damn*, it hurts! What the *hell* are you laughin' at?"

"The biggest horse's ass that ever rode under the Lone Star, that's what. Touch your head."

Rip did, gingerly at first. "Great jumpin' Judas! It's all there! Fargo, you hairy-headed chicken-plucker, what the hell is goin' on?"

"It was all just a bad dream, old son."

"Bad dream, my sweet aunt! Here's some hair layin' on my blanket. Fargo, the hell you been up to?"

It was a good question, and the smile faded from Fargo's lips. Especially with reliable Cherokees waiting in the wings, he had no desire to enlist Comanches on his side. They were good fighters, all right, but they were also too volatile and unstable. Yet, his position here in the Indian Territory was too weak to send them packing. He was neither up the well nor down, and if he didn't handle this new stick of dynamite carefully, it would blow up in his face.

"What have I been up to?" he finally replied. "Rip, I'm afraid I just made a deal with the devil, which means we just might have hell to pay."

12

Two tallow candles burned on a broad plank placed over two empty nail kegs, illuminating a dingy, dirt-floored room. It was poorly and sparsely furnished: four crude shakedowns for sleeping, a three-legged stool, and a split-log bench pulled up to the plank table.

"Do you think Justin is trying to help us, Rebecca?" Louise Starr asked a fellow captive.

"I should smile he is!" Rebecca Halfpenny retorted, her comment immediately followed by a hacking cough. "But I just don't see much he can do. He's a good man, but he's no killer like these double-poxed hounds who are holding us."

Louise wore a blue broadcloth dress and a muslin apron, and still possessed some of the pretty looks her daughter Belinda inherited from her. "I fear the same thing. Besides, he knows you—*all* of us—will be killed if he doesn't do their bidding. That's a lot of pressure on any man."

"Or woman," Joshua Starr chimed in, closing a calfskin Bible that sat on the crude table. "Our Belinda has it even worse than Justin because she has to endure—"

"Josh," his wife cut him off. "Little pitchers have big ears."

Scotty Starr, just a stripling of eleven years, sat on the stool listlessly trying to spin a top in the dirt. His rough homespun shirt was filthy, and his corduroy pants patched with old flour sacking.

"I know what Pa means," he told the three adults. "I hope this fellow Sis told us about kills *all* these sons of—"

"Scotty!" Louise snapped. "We don't have to sink to their level."

"If we sink any more," the lad told her, "we'll come out in China."

"It's all my fault," Joshua said bitterly. "This Fargo is risking his life, yet I don't even have the guts to give the Winslowe brothers the rough side of my tongue."

"Well, that's smart," Rebecca insisted. Her thin, sharp-nosed face looked like yellowed ivory in the candlelight.

"Very smart," Louise agreed. "Dear, they'd just kill you."

"Willing to wound but afraid to strike—that's me," Joshua said, his tone sharply bitter. "A broken-down hoeman from Ohio who thought he was smarter than the rest. Oh, *what* have I done to us all?"

"Josh, what's done is done," Louise insisted. "You can't change anything by constantly blaming yourself."

Joshua reached into his hip pocket and pulled out a map printed on onionskin paper. "Right there it is, Louise, in black-and-white: the Red River Cutoff. Oh, Lord, we were *cut off*, all right."

He wadded the useless map into a ball and threw it on the floor. "Used to, a man could count on the next fellow to practice the Golden Rule. Nowadays, the gold just rules."

"And it's bean soup once a day," Scotty complained. "I'm hungry."

"We've got some salt meat Belinda sneaked in," Louise reminded her son. "Trouble is, it makes a body thirsty, and we never have enough water."

Rebecca shook with another coughing spasm. "It would be easier to put up with all that," she said in a weak voice after it passed, "if it didn't feel like we're living in the inside of a boot. No windows, no doors, forced to bury our night soil in the dirt like cats—I don't even know when it's night or day unless Belinda tells us. At least a caged animal can see out."

Her words were so true they left everyone sitting in gloomy silence. Louise Starr, ever the voice of pioneer optimism, finally broke it.

"'Tis a long lane that has no turning. Help *will* come."

When Fargo guessed, by the angle of the polestar, that it was midnight, he and Rip began tacking their horses.

"Damn it, Fargo, this jerked buffalo and parched corn lays heavy on my chest," Rip griped. "We need meat—fresh meat."

"Are you soft-brained? We got no time to hunt, and we can't

expose ourselves like that. When I was scouting earlier, I spotted several riders looking for us."

"I said nothing," Rip protested, "about hunting. Only thing to hunt around here is buffalo, and it's usually the bulls who wander into this area from the herds to the north. The meat of a bull buffalo is the worstest thing I ever et 'cept for elk—so dry it's like chewin' cotton."

"If you happen to wander near a point," Fargo told him as he cinched the girth, "feel free to make it."

"Can't we mebbe snare a rabbit near the cave?"

"That's not a bad idea. Rabbit meat's a little greasy, but it's not bad if you scorch it. No jackrabbits, though."

"*God* no," Rip agreed. "I made a stew from one once that coulda puked a buzzard off a gut wagon."

They led their mounts outside into the chilly night air. It was warmer farther to the south, and heat lightning flashed on the horizon.

"Bright night," Rip complained. "Full moon, starry sky, and no clouds. Not like last night."

"If we only rode out when *you* said it was safe," Fargo said, "we'd never leave the cave."

Fargo took a careful squint around; then they forked leather and headed down the bluff toward the river.

"You know, Fargo, that damn water will be colder than a witch's tit this time of night. Why not just ride in from this side?"

"Because we can't. The sandbar willows are the only good place to hide our horses on this side, and they know we used them last night. They'll likely be watching them."

"Mebbe there's nothin' on the Texas side, neither."

"I scouted it," Fargo reminded him. "About one mile east of the outlaw settlement there's a thick stand of tall brush."

"Well, hell. They can check that, too."

Fargo shook his head. "Could, but won't. The lazy trash working for Winslowe won't want to ford in this chill."

"That shines, but is it smart to go back this soon? They'll be lookin' for us."

"Rip, you are some piece of work. You tell all these tales about riding with Captain Coleman and killing Mexicans and Apaches by the wagonload, yet this ride tonight puts ice in your boots?"

"*Tales*, huh? So now you're callin' me a liar?"

"No, not exactly a liar. Like most Texans, you remember big."

Rip chuckled. "Ahuh, I do tell a stretcher now and agin. So what are we after tonight?"

"For one thing, I just want to see how they're reacting to last night—what kind of guard they've set up and that type of deal. I also hope to talk to Justin about that cannon. If he knows where it is, and gives me the tools, I can spike it. Here we are—time to swim."

They reached the grassy bank of Red River, it's quick surface reflecting like a million shimmering diamonds in the moonlight, and swung down. They loosened the girths a notch, so their horses could breathe easier in the water, and forded easily except for the bracing shock of cold water.

They rode fast for a couple miles to dry out, then reined in to a trot, Fargo's vigilant eyes missing nothing in the moonlight.

"Fargo?"

"Yeah?"

"What happened to the horny old couple who couldn't tell the difference between lubricating grease and putty?"

"I don't know."

"Their windows fell out."

Fargo snorted. "That's not as funny as watching you get scalped this morning."

"Oh, that was a barrel of monks, all right. Say, I always heard tell how the Trailsman is real particular who he ties to. But he'll let murderin' Comanches side him? Why not just shove a rattlesnake down your pants?"

"Never mind, and pipe down so I can listen. That stand of brush is just ahead."

Fargo went on ahead to make sure it was safe, then whistled Rip forward. The Trailsman swung his leg over the cantle and dismounted, landing light as a cat. Both men led their horses deeper into cover, dropped the bridles, and hobbled their mounts.

Reluctantly, Fargo left his Henry in the saddle scabbard—it would be an encumbrance for tonight's job. Unlike last night, they would not have the element of surprise, and if caught, only rapid escape would save them.

"We'll have to hoof it for about fifteen minutes," he said.

"And we'll have to get soaked again when we cross the river. Before we do, give me your dragoon so I can throw it over— otherwise the powder loads will get wet."

"I'm done fightin' you, Fargo," Rip assured him. "You know what you're up to—I guess a well-bred dog hunts by nature. But don't forget these boys is rarin' to kill you."

"Yeah, me and my grizzled old pard, so keep your nose to the wind."

Fargo realized, even before drawing even with the outlaw hell-hole on the opposite bank, that they would have to ford well past the settlement. Several bonfires blazed, including one where a sentry sat right next to the water, resting his back against a cot-tonwood.

"Jesus Christ and various saints," Rip whispered as they crouched in the deep grass. "The place is lit up like a gambling parlor. Worse luck."

"No, *our* luck," Fargo whispered back. "Notice how that guard is gazing right into the fire?"

"Ahuh. Prob'ly dreamin' of all the pretty girls he's raped and killed."

"The point, chucklehead, is that he's ruining his night vision. The rest are just as ignorant and likely doing the same. Should make it easier for us to move around."

Thanks to the bright night and the large fires, Fargo could clearly see the gloomy clump of mud hovels, brush shanties, tar-papered shacks, and clapboard shebangs. The trading post with its log wall sat like a fort at the east end of this hardcase den.

Fargo was about to head farther upriver when a voice called out, "Yo, Harlan!"

"Who's that?" responded the sentry near the river. Fargo and Rip pressed even flatter into the grass.

"It's Alsey."

"All right, c'mon down."

Alsey moved down the sloping bank, a shadowy figure dressed in black.

"Chuck that butt, you damn fool," Harlan snapped. "You're giving Fargo an easy target."

Alsey flicked his cigarette into the water. "Any trouble?"

"Just these goddamn skeeters eating me alive. Your end quiet?"

"Like a farm town on Sunday," Alsey replied. "It's like I told Stone—Fargo ain't stupid enough to come here two nights in a row."

"Sure he is," Rip whispered in Fargo's ear.

"All I know," Harlan said, "is that I don't like the turns this trail is taking. First Stone stops greasing our palms like he used to. Now we're getting shot up by the Trailsman. Who *wouldn't* ride the owlhoot trail?"

"No women, the grub stinks, and a man can't even get a shave," Alsey added. "Meantime, Stone spends his nights in dry shelter poking that fine little heifer from Ohio. You noticed the *tits* on that little piece?"

"How could I miss them? Talk about puffy loaves . . . anyhow, I'm ready to get shut of this job. Some of the boys are talking about joining these border gangs back in Kansas and Missouri. They ride into a town and take any women they want."

Alsey said, "Brother, that sounds like it's right up my road. But Stone promises more money soon's we sack this next keelboat. I got warrants on my ass, so I reckon I'll stick here a mite longer."

"Same here, but only if we put the quietus on Fargo. Ain't nothing more bothersome than a goddamn crusader."

"All right, Harlan, keep your eyes open. I'll check back with you in about an hour."

Alsey headed back up the bank.

"Just like you predicted," Rip whispered. "The rats is unhappy and about to abandon ship."

"Maybe, maybe not," Fargo whispered back. "Outlaws are like soldiers—they complain from get-up to go-to-bed."

Staying behind low bushes as much as possible, both men moved about fifty yards upriver. The Red was narrow enough for Fargo to flip the dragoon across in an underhand toss. Then, once again, they endured the numbing chill of the water as they swam across.

"Wait here until I give you the hoot," Fargo told his shivering partner. "It'll be an hour before Alsey comes back, so I might's well put Harlan out of commission and sink his weapons."

"Ahuh. And from what we heard, happens Alsey finds his pard stove up, mebbe they'll *both* light a shuck out of here—convincing a few others before they leave."

"I'll work on that," Fargo promised.

He drew the Arkansas toothpick from his boot and cat-footed silently forward. Fargo hooked around behind the tree, watching Harlan the way a hawk watches prey. The man was pallid and stout with a melting chin and a soft, lopsided mouth.

Harlan emitted a hissing gasp when Fargo put the lethal point of the Arkansas toothpick against his neck.

Fargo stepped into full view. "Recognize me, Harlan?"

The outlaw nodded once, on the verge of blubbering. His Adam's apple bobbed up and down as he fought to find his voice. "Please, mister, don't kill me. I'm just a nickel-chaser. Stone Winslowe is—"

"Stick a sock in it and lissen up. Stone Winslowe will soon burn in hell, and so will any low-crawling snake that works for him. The next time I see you in these parts, I'll blow your brains out the back of your goddamn skull. *Comprende?*"

"Yessir, I understand."

"Good," Fargo said, shucking out his Colt and bringing the barrel down hard on Harlan's forehead. The man slumped unconscious.

Fargo removed the man's filthy neckerchief and gagged him with it, then untied Harlan's rope belt and used it to tie his wrists together behind the tree. It was quick work to toss his Jennings rifle and Remington six-gun into the middle of the river.

Fargo gave the owl hoot, and Rip joined him, dragoon at the ready.

"Cut his damn throat," Rip urged.

"Killing I'm all right with, old son. But murder sticks in my craw. That would put me in with the rest of this trash."

"Why you pickin' up them stones?" Rip asked.

"You'll see. Follow me, and stick close."

Fargo bore east, toward the trading-post compound. He and Rip stayed in the shadow of the log wall, for at least two bonfires were burning in the pig wallow that passed for a street. Fargo noticed the former saloons were piles of charred ashes, but a crude plank bar had been set up in front of the old Sawdust Corner.

"Look at them sons of whores," Rip muttered, meaning the congregation of riffraff milling around the bar like flies around a molasses barrel.

Fargo had noticed, during his first trip here, that Justin lived in the smithy. But as he'd expected, the gate was closed and no doubt watched from within.

"We'll have to hide in those trees across the way," Fargo said. "It's too bright here. If those bastards weren't so shellacked, they'd've spotted us already."

The moment Fargo fell silent, a gun opened up with a hammering racket that made Fargo's blood run cold. His Colt leaped into his fist. Then he realized it was just a drunk shooting at the moon.

"Now!" he told Rip, racing across the primitive street.

Both men made it into the shadows. Fargo began tossing stones over the wall, aiming them at the canvas roof of the smithy. After a half dozen tosses, the gate meowed open and Justin's shaggy head appeared around it.

"Justin!" Fargo called out in a low but urgent voice. "Over here. It's two friends. If you're allowed out, c'mon over."

Looking hesitant but curious, the involuntary blacksmith hurried over to join them.

"Mr. Fargo!" he exclaimed when he recognized the Trailsman. "Have you lost your buttons? If you two want to stay healthy, best dust your hocks out of here. After last night, they want your guts for garters."

"Yeah, I see their guards and fires," Fargo said. "But are any of them getting cold feet?"

Justin nodded. "Stone's had a corncob up his ass all day because three men crossed into Texas and got the hell out. With that, plus the four that's been killed, he can't afford to lose many more men."

Even in the shadows, Fargo could see how forlorn Justin looked. His grain-sack trousers hardly qualified as rags.

"I know I look like hell," he said, as if plucking the thought from Fargo's mind. "Men like you can take care of themselves, but for me, life without a woman is powerful rough. I talked to Belinda, and she told me you know about our people being prisoners."

"Do you get to visit your wife?" Fargo asked.

He shook his head. "I wish to God I could. Rebecca's poorly, Mr. Fargo. Consumptive. Belinda takes them food once a day, is all."

"Once a day!" Rip echoed. "Why, that's slow starvation."

"Honest to John, Mr. Fargo, I *wanted* to tell you all about it on that first day you two gents rode in. But me and Belinda got us a . . . whatchacallit, a pact to stay mum. You know about them now, but please don't ask me to say *where* they are."

"I won't," Fargo promised. "But maybe you can tell me where something else is—that cannon. I'd like to spike the barrel."

"They don't trust me to know where they hide it. All I know is that it was brought here on a big keelboat by Caswell Jones."

A sudden flutter of hooves, from the west, sent all three men crouching. Bradford Winslowe, his four-inch rowels glinting in the moonlight, hauled back on the reins and leaped to the ground to open the gate. Fargo saw fresh blood on the bay's flanks.

Bradford disappeared inside, and Rip muttered, "There's one son of a bitch that needs killing."

"Plenty have tried to douse his light," Justin said, "and he's sent every one of them to hunt for the white buffalo. He's been out looking for you, Mr. Fargo."

"Is he likely to turn in now?" Fargo asked. "Or will he leave the trading post again?"

"He doesn't stay there. Only Stone does. The rest of the brothers just keep their horses there."

The news startled Fargo. He hadn't asked Belinda about it, carelessly assuming all the brothers stayed in the compound.

"Where *are* Bradford and Bo staying?" he asked.

Justin pointed toward the sod house with a dwarf cliff as its back wall. It sat by itself, farther back from the street. From its age and solid walls, Fargo guessed that wintering trappers might have built it twenty or thirty years ago.

"Bradford's been out looking for you all day," Justin explained. "I think Bo's out walking patrol with that fancy killing rifle. He's teched in the head with the revenge need since you killed his brother Clint."

Fargo squinted. "Somebody's cut a few windows in the soddy. There appears to be some light in there, but it could just be from those bonfires."

"Oh, hell," Rip muttered. "Fargo's brain is at work—stand by for the blast."

"Mr. Fargo," Justin said earnestly, "I ain't took part in none of the killings. I swear to God, I ain't."

"Hell, we know that, Justin."

"They force me to drive the plunder wagon or make repairs when it breaks down. It made me sick to my belly watching them murder those three teamsters a week or so back. I'll hang for sure."

"Like hell you will," Fargo scoffed. "You'll never even go to court. Law doesn't hold a man to account for crimes he was forced to commit. Frankly, I doubt if these crimes will ever even be prosecuted, given where they happened. If they are, I'll make sure the truth gets out."

"Assumin' *you* survive this," Rip chimed in.

"I always assume that, worrywart," Fargo said. "Justin, you best mosey along now before they get too suspicious."

"Yes, sir. Before I go, is there anything you need me to do? I'm no leader, but I take orders good. Leastways, I hope I can."

"For now," Fargo said, "just keep your ears open and don't upset the chuck wagon. While they hold those captives, you have to toe the line."

Justin shook both men's hands. "Good luck. Those Winslowes mean to kill all of us when they're done here, so you're placing no one at risk but yourselves. God bless brave men!"

"Hell, he ain't no war chief," Rip said as they watched the blacksmith start back toward the trading post, "but I like that jasper."

"Seems like a good man," Fargo agreed. "The steady and faithful type the West could use more of. He's worried sick over his wife, poor fellow."

Justin was about halfway across the fire-lit street when Fargo heard the sound he'd been dreading all night: the high-percussion crack of that customized Spencer rifle. Simultaneously, Justin's hatless head literally exploded, and the lifeless body took one more shambling step before collapsing to the ground, toes scratching the dirt a few times as his nervous system tried to deny the fact of death.

13

"Well, bleedin' Holy Ghost!" Rip cried out, starting to lunge toward Justin's fallen body.

"Shut pan and stay down," Fargo ordered, pulling the old-timer back. "He's past help, and we're better off staying put."

"I killed Fargo, boys!" Bo Winslowe's voice shouted.

"Like hob, you did!" another voice replied. "It's Halfpenny."

"Christ! He hardly ever goes past the gate."

"Did you spot any muzzle fire?" Rip asked.

Rage gripped Fargo so tightly it left his jaw aching. "Yeah. The right-hand window of that sod house. Justin must have been wrong about Bo being out patrolling."

"Ahuh. I figured it had to be Bo on account Bradford's in the trading post. You think he knew he was shooting at Halfpenny?"

"Damned if I know," Fargo replied. "Sounds like a bone-headed mistake. It can't be because he knew we were here, or he'd've sounded the alarm."

Bo stayed in the house, but several men had congregated around the dead man, Bradford joining them from the trading post.

"Jesus, Bo," he called to his brother, "why'd you kill our only blacksmith? He was just probably coming back from taking a crap."

"Ain't my fault the light was tricky. From this angle he looked like Fargo."

"You trigger-happy fool, are you moon-crazy? We lost a good worker."

Bradford squatted to study the damage. "Well, it was a hum-dinger of a shot, anyhow. Blew half his brains out. Just like I taught you, little brother—only a head shot guarantees an instant kill."

Bradford stood up and holstered his shooter. "You two, Corey and Dexter. Drag that corpse down to the river and toss it in. I don't want the stink around here—puts me off my feed. Then get back on guard and patrolling. And remember—we want Fargo *captured*, if possible, not killed. He done for my brother Clint, and his last sight in this world will be me looking at him down a gun barrel before I shoot him low in the guts to make him suffer."

Fargo did a slow boil while the body was dragged away like trash. The rest of the men drifted off.

"Puts him off his feed," Rip repeated. "That son of a bitch could walk under a snake's belly on stilts."

"That describes all the Winslowe brothers," Fargo said, his mouth a grim, determined slit. "Including the one that's going to die tonight."

Rip's jaw dropped open. "You're going to kill Bo? Ain't that what *you* call murder?"

Fargo shucked out his Colt and rolled the cylinder against his palm, checking the action. "Who did he think he was murdering just now?"

"You."

"Right. Instead, he murdered the wrong man. So it's murder no matter how you slice it. Besides, I won't blindside him—I'll give him an even break."

"What—"

Fargo waved him quiet. "This is no time to discuss the causes of the wind. You wait right here while I reconnoiter the house. I won't take long."

Fargo moved to the edge of the tree cover and peered right, toward the makeshift thirst parlor. Fewer men stood around the fire now, but the flames were brighter. Hating to do it, but leery of creating a profile, he dropped down and rolled across the debris-strewn street.

When he reached the east front corner of the soddy, he rose to his knees and carefully peeked over the edge of a crude window in the side of the structure. There had never been glass in the space, and ragged tatters were all that was left of the oiled paper that once covered it.

Immediately he spotted the source of the faint light: a small candle burning atop an old barrel. Two men sat on old dry-goods boxes, using the barrel as a table for their poker game. Old planks divided the soddy into two rooms. An archway into the second room showed Bo sitting intently at a window opening in the front of the soddy, giving him an excellent view of the street outside.

The bored-out Spencer rifle lay across his thighs. Fargo couldn't help realizing, as he returned to Rip's position, that he was extremely vulnerable from the house. Even as he anticipated the Spencer's deadly crack, he reminded himself: *You never hear the shot that kills you.*

"All right," he greeted Rip, "here's how we're going to play it . . ."

Fargo crouched under the side window and bided his time. He knew he could shoot the two gamblers, but then Bo would leap out of sight. Men would come running at the sound of gunfire, so his play had to be quick. That meant his only choice was to assume the gamblers would leave soon.

One of the card players, a huge redhead wearing an eye patch, called out, "Say, Bo?"

"Yeah?"

"Now that Halfpenny has gone up the flume, can I have first dibs on his woman? You and your brothers won't need her no more."

"Little old for you, ain't she, Boone?"

"My pap use to say, if they still got teeth, they're still juicy."

The other player, a beanpole of a man with teeth like crooked yellow tombstones, said, "That bitch is a lunger, Boone. Coughs every thirty seconds."

"So what? I don't kiss 'em, anyhow. How 'bout it, Bo? Them older gals know how to use it."

"We'll see, we'll see. I'll talk to Stone. We don't need you boys scrappin' over her like dogs over meat. Say, ain't that 'short break' of yours about over?"

"Damn you, Marty!" Boone snapped at the human beanpole. "That's U.S. script you just slapped down—that's for soldiers. I want money that *spends*."

"Talk to Stone," Marty retorted. "Ain't been no mazuma lately."

"There'll be plenty of money," Bo called from the second room, "for them as ain't scared of one man."

"It's easy to kill an unarmed blacksmith," Boone taunted as he slapped down a card. "This Fargo is a different kettle of fish."

"I'll grant that his clover's been deep, so far. But it's time for the worm to turn."

"Speaking of money," Marty said, "why'n't you come in here and play a few hands. The deck ain't marked."

"Table stakes or limit game?"

"Table stakes."

"Forget it," Bo said. "That's too rich for my blood. Stone might be my brother, but he don't give me no more than he pays you fellows. Besides, I figure Fargo's going to show up, and I plan to be his welcoming committee."

"He ain't no fool," Boone scoffed. "Last night nobody expected him—tonight he's walking into a stacked deck."

Fargo heard running footsteps approach and pressed flat against the side of the soddy.

"Bo!" shouted a man out in the street. Fargo recognized one of the outlaws who had been ordered to toss Justin's corpse into the river. "Fargo's here! We just found Harlan tied to a tree. He was conked hard on the head and he's still groggy, so he can't tell us much."

Fargo heard Bo swear. "So he ain't no fool, huh, Boone? I *told* you Fargo would come. All right, Corey, go tell Stone and Bradford he's here."

Fargo heard Bo step into the nearest room. "You two been shuffling them pasteboards long enough. This ain't no time for lollygagging, what with Fargo on the loose. One of you go hide up the trail in case they head out toward the bluffs. The other hide by the river. We've got men all over, and them two cock-chafers will *not* slip through the net."

"You going with us, Bo?"

"You been grazing loco weed? I got the best weapon in town, and the best vantage point to use it from. Fargo's a bold son of a bitch who likes to take the bull by the horns, and I still think he'll show himself right around here. Blow out that damn candle."

Both men left, and Fargo heard Bo's stool scrape the packed-dirt floor as he resumed his position. Fargo had one remaining problem: he couldn't count on climbing in the window, crossing the room, and getting the drop on Bo without being spotted in the man's side vision. He needed a diversion at the window to Bo's left, and that's where Rip came in.

Fargo signaled across the street to the position where Rip was hiding in the trees, hoping the old-timer was on the qui vive. He was—he darted out of the trees immediately, staying wide to avoid Bo's line of sight. Fargo was gratified to note that only two men remained at the nearest bonfire, their night vision too ruined by bright flames to notice the old man crawling under Bo's front window to round the corner of the house.

"Say, Bo? It's Alsey. You got a match?"

The moment Bo's head swiveled toward the window, Fargo climbed inside, thumbed back the Colt's hammer without clearing leather, and moved quickly to close with the other man. Rip stood to one side of the window opening.

"Alsey, the *hell* you doing standing around with your dick in your hand? Never mind the smoke, Fargo's been spotted. You're on roving patrol, so get thrashing."

Bo, his panther-scarred cheek visible in the bright moonlight and sawing flames, looked out the window again.

Here comes your even break, bastard, Fargo thought, again hearing Justin's toes scratching the dirt like some frenzied animal. *Don't take it.*

"Bo," he said softly.

The man started violently, realizing his dilemma even before he glanced right to confirm it was Fargo standing there like the Angel of Death.

Don't take it, Fargo wished again, and an eyeblink later he got his wish when Bo, snarling like a rabid cur, swung the Spencer toward him.

Quicker than eyesight Fargo filled his hand. An orange spear-tip of flame spat from the Colt's muzzle, and a neat hole appeared in Bo's forehead, a long rope of blood spurting from it. The rifle thumped to the floor, and Bo toppled after it like a sack of potatoes.

"Sorry to spoil your big time," Fargo told the corpse before he grabbed the rifle and ducked out the open door.

Thanks to his gunshot Fargo knew time was of the essence now, just as he knew it was foolish to try escaping right now.

Rip had followed orders and returned to their hiding place in the trees across the street. But before Fargo could join him, he had to create the impression that they were fleeing by the river route.

He sent a round toward the two sentries by the bonfire, who immediately opened fire on him. Bullets wind-tickling him, Fargo made sure they saw him run south toward the river.

"Check in both directions along the bank!" he heard Bradford shout. "Their horses have to be close by!"

With the manpower thus sent on a wild-goose chase, Fargo ran north again and joined Rip in the trees.

"I take it Bo's worm fodder now?" Rip greeted him.

"Dead as a Paiute grave," Fargo confirmed.

"Bradford's gonna have him a hissy fit now. It's just him and Stone left."

"The madder he gets," Fargo replied, "the better I like it. It's the cool head that wins the campaign."

"That shines. But was it smart to hole up here?"

"*Smart?* Hell, if we were smart we'd be back in St. Joe outfitting pilgrims for the Oregon Trail. But I figure we're reasonably safe here—after all, they think I just escaped along the river. Still, we'd best take turnabout on guard duty, and for Christ sakes, *don't* nod out when it's your spell."

"I won't—I'm sober, more's the pity. When do we light out—daybreak?"

"Just before. These owlhoots are putting in a long night," Fargo said. "With luck, they'll bed down by then."

"Say," Rip exclaimed, just now noticing the rifle. "You took that fancy thunder stick from Bo."

The Spencer's modifications included a removable magazine in place of the usual trap in the butt plate. Fargo released it and pulled out the bullets.

"It's a full load," he said. "Eleven rounds instead of the usual seven."

Rip took one of the rounds and squinted to study it. "Say, these ain't the same copper-jacketed slugs that get stuck in the breech. Bigger powder load, too."

"Yeah. The only drawback is that we can't reload it with any of our ammo. But with this scope and the larger powder loads, this little puppy could deal some misery."

"It sure's hell has so far," Rip said, his tone grim. "Ask Justin.

But you avenged that, and when these peckerwoods find Bo, ought to be some more yellow-bellied skunks hightailing it."

"Let's hope so," Fargo said. "The trouble is, Stone is getting desperate to hold this pack of rat bastards together, and that means an attack on Etienne and the voyageurs sooner rather than later."

"Ahuh, and you say the boat crew's got good weapons they can't use worth a shit?"

"In a nutshell," Fargo replied. "Ain't it grand to be alive?"

14

Fargo's knowledge of criminal laziness—and criminal cowardice—proved right once again. Well before dawn the drunks had passed out, and even the men who were still sober were asleep around the bonfires, grouping together in case Fargo and his grizzled partner returned. Even Bradford and Stone, struck speechless by the death of a second brother, had merely hauled Bo's body into the compound and locked the gate.

The men left on guard duty at the nearest fire nodded off around five a.m. This allowed the two intruders in the trees to slip down to the mist-shrouded river without incident and quickly ford, Fargo wading into the fast, bracing current as far as he could before tossing the dragoon and the Spencer onto the opposite bank.

The mist made visibility poor as they covered the mile to their secreted horses, but Fargo's ears picked up the dull thud of hooves just in time. He pulled Rip to cover in a thicket as a rider wearing a long black duster trotted past, a sawed-off scattergun resting in the crook of his left arm. It was only a little after sunrise when both men returned to the cave. Cold, hungry, and bone weary, they peeled out of their wet clothes, gnawed on some jerky, then rolled into their blankets for a few hours sleep.

Fargo woke up before noon and kicked Rip's foot. "Roust out, Methuselah. This ain't no old-pensioners' home."

Rip woke up in a bragging mood. "Talk about your hair-breadth escapes! Fargo, we harrowed hell itself and got out alive. I defied death right alongside the Trailsman. No, sir! You won't find Ranger Rip Miller hiding in *his* tipi when the war whoop sounds."

"Not hiding—drunk and asleep."

"Christ, Fargo, you got enough mouth for three lips, know

111

that? All that asleep on guard duty business is smoke behind us. Don't you *never* let a thing go? 'To err is human, to forgive divine.' Ain't you heard that?"

"Good," said Fargo. "Then God can forgive you because I won't."

"Ahh . . . say, speakin' of bein' drunk, I wish I had me some forty-rod. I'm about to get the jim-jams."

"You get the tremors," Fargo warned him, "and I'll shoot you. I'll tolerate no deadweight."

Fargo went outside and hid in the rock tumble, studying the river valley below him. He spotted an outrider from the outlaw haven and it troubled him. This was the first time he'd seen one this far east—was he spying on the keelboat downriver? Fargo determined to visit it today.

Before he went inside again, Fargo checked Rip's snare and found a plump rabbit. He bled, skinned, and rough-gutted it before dressing it out. He used his knife to bury the entrails, then washed his hands in the sand.

"All right, hashslinger," he said when he returned to the cave. "Recruit that fire and cook us some meat."

Rip's eyes widened. "*Now* we'll eat like by-god white men! Lemme have your toothpick."

He built up the fire. Then, using Fargo's knife as a spit, he turned the rabbit slowly over the flames.

"I haven't seen any Comanches since Medicine Flute left here yesterday," Fargo remarked. "I wonder what they're up to."

"I'd wager they're out attacking road ranches in Texas," Rip surmised, meaning way stations for the Overland line. "That, and killing express riders, is their favorite sport. And *you* want to ride with 'em."

"The ass waggeth his ears," Fargo retorted. "If I'd said no, we'd both be marked for a nameless grave. Anyhow, with luck we'll put them to good use."

"You wanna spell that out?"

"I'll tell you when it's a plan. Right now it's just an idea."

"Comanches," Rip said, "are so evil that quicksand would spit them back up. Still, I'd like to see some of the peaceful tribes around here prosper. But The Nations will fail for the same damn reason the Republic of Texas went under: no money and too many factional battles. Jammin' all these tribes together is like tossin' a dozen cats into one sack."

"I'll have to second that," Fargo said. "Hell, Rip, I guess even a blind hog will root up an acorn now and then."

"Fargo, you don't kick a pullin' mule," Rip warned. "I'm cookin' your dinner, ain't I?"

"Right as the mail. I apologize, old son."

"But speakin' of evil tribes," Rip nattered on, "once I was jumped by Bannocks below the Great Bend of the Carson. Them red sons like to burn a white man alive. I scairt 'em off by actin' like a crazy man—tore off my clothes and jumped around like one a them great apes in the jungle, howlin' and gruntin' and beatin' my chest. They figure it's bad medicine to kill a crazy man, so they lit a shuck outta there."

"That story I believe," Fargo assured him. "Seeing *you* naked would scare any man sick and silly."

"Go piss up a rope." Rip tore off a piece of the charred meat and handed it to Fargo. "This'll stay your belly."

Both men were ravenous and tied into the meat for several minutes.

"This one's a dilly," Rip said, still chewing. "This sheriff is makin' the rounds when he hears moaning and thrashin' from the bushes at the edge of town. He parts the bushes and catches this naked couple makin' the two-backed beast. Well, the young fellow starts sweatin' to beat hell.

"'Please, sheriff,' he begs, 'don't arrest us. We ain't doin' no harm.' 'Relax, son,' the sheriff says. 'You just let me have seconds, and I'll forget all about this.' Hearin' that, the young fellow gets even more nervous and starts shakin'.'Why, son, what are you scared of?' the sheriff asks.

"'Oh, I ain't scared, sir. It's just—I never screwed a sheriff before.'"

Rip shook with laughter at his own joke, meat spraying from his mouth. Fargo, however, seemed hardly to hear it—only a faint shadow of a smile touched his lips.

Rip scowled. "You must have a burr under your saddle, Fargo. That's a good joke."

"I thought so, too, the first time I heard it—ten years ago."

"Hell, I just repeat 'em—I don't make up new ones."

Fargo finished eating and wiped his hands on his buckskins. "Never mind jokes. We're riding east later to talk to Etienne. First I'm riding out to take a squint around. I got a god-fear that Stone won't wait for that keelboat to set sail. This cur named Caswell Jones is coming any day now, and Stone owes him a full load. Men are deserting, and Stone needs money to keep them around."

While Fargo rigged the Ovaro, Rip said in a regretful tone: "I know I can't stay here for good, Trailsman, but I like holing up in this cave by myself. I shoulda been a mountain man. I got no use for friends and all the damn favors they ask of a body. A friend in need is a friend to feed, so piss on 'em."

Fargo buckled the bridle. "That's might tall talk coming from a man who had to be dragged out from under a dead horse."

"Hell, I was ready to die. 'Sides, it was a stranger what pulled me out, not a friend."

"Well, I'm your friend now, you cantankerous son of a bitch," Fargo said, leading his stallion toward the cave entrance.

"No need to slop over," Rip said gruffly, though he looked pleased.

"Make sure the powder loads in your dragoon haven't clumped," Fargo advised. "And keep that Spencer handy with a round in the chamber. Stone Winslowe's bootlicks are patrolling more, and you might have uninvited company."

Fargo rode east to the low end of the bluff, then gave the Ovaro his head and let him ride down to the river, sure-footed as a mountain goat. Curious to know how heavy human traffic was, this close to the cave, he rode down to a nearby sandbar and studied it.

The dusty twang of grasshoppers' wings gave the day a lazy feel, but Fargo wasn't lulled by it. He saw plenty of fresh animal tracks, which wouldn't be there in such numbers if men had been around recently. As he rode along the grassy bank, eyes in constant motion, bobwhites and jays, in nearby stands of dogwood, scolded this human intruder.

Fargo's experienced eyes read the terrain as if it were a book telling a story. Now and then he found faint vestiges of hoofprints made by horses, some shod, some unshod. Most were old, a fact he determined by how far the pressed grass had sprung back up.

"Whoa, old campaigner," he said abruptly, tugging rein and staring at the grass to his left.

A line of prints had flattened the lush grass—prints of two riders, and so recent that only a few blades of grass had started to spring up. Fargo started to follow them, then realized they led into a blackthorn thicket about thirty yards to his left.

Two sets of prints riding in, none coming out.

In the next few moments, quick reflexes and a superb horse saved Fargo's life. At the same moment that he heard the metallic snick of a rifle being cocked, he slapped the Ovaro's neck, and the stallion shot ahead like an arrow from a bow. The hidden rifle spoke its piece, and Fargo heard a bullet snap past just behind his head.

A second rifle pitched into the game, and bullets pestered him like angry wasps as Fargo put his chin in the mane and fled downriver. He did not need to spur the bullet-savvy Ovaro on— this was familiar sport to the pinto, who went from dead stop to dead run in a matter of seconds.

When the Ovaro's mane was matted with sweat, Fargo reined in to a trot, knowing he was well out of rifle range and well beyond any pursuers. But there weren't any—Fargo slued around for a look back and saw two riders retreating west at a breakneck pace. Typical behavior for outlaws firing from ambush.

"Nice work, boy," Fargo told his stallion. "If we get out of this country alive, I'll make sure you get plenty of crushed barley."

Fargo decided to loop north and approach the cave obliquely in case he was still being watched. Despite the successful escape, he felt a familiar bitterness tinged with sadness. This was just one more reminder that the days of saddles and spurs and wide-open ranges would soon enough give way to even more criminal predators, to trains and cities, to fences and factories, to creek banks lined with placer mines, to mountains denuded of timber.

And soon he would be driven out by those who used the very trails he blazed, used them to overrun him with taxes and lawyers and shady "New York land speculators"—the kind who, like Stone Winslowe, were looking to get rich off someone else's labor and risks. But always, a determined defiance kept Fargo pushing past the next ridge.

"Always running from cussed syphillization," he said aloud, and the Ovaro nickered as if agreeing.

Fargo gave the owl hoot so Rip wouldn't shoot him as he entered the cave.

"Where you been?" Rip greeted him. "Bust your leg in a badger hole?"

"Had a little set-to with ambushers," Fargo replied, leading the Ovaro back to the seep spring. He had led the stallion in for the last half hour, cooling him out so he'd be fresh for another ride.

"Winslowe's hired guns?" Rip demanded.

"I didn't get a good look at 'em, but it had to be. They bore due west toward their rats' nest."

"I thought I heard shots," Rip fretted. "Mebbe they're closing in on us. Hell, that Comanche found us."

Fargo dropped the Ovaro's bridle so he could drink. "Don't go by that Comanche—it's likely he already knew about this place. But Stone's bunch prob'ly are closing in. Either we bring this thing to a head quick, or we're back to cold camps on the plains."

"Don't make a nevermind to me," Rip said. "I like this cave. Keeps the horses hid, and we can have fires. But now that I know Comanches know about it, I can't never roost here agin."

Fargo began checking his cinches and latigos. "Bosh. You got nothing they want. These are renegade raiders looking for spoils. They'll take children and young women as slaves, but you're just a mouth to feed."

"What's your drift?" Rip bristled.

Fargo laughed. "I believe my point was clear, Methuselah. I see your scrub is already rigged. Let's make tracks."

"Speakin' of Comanches and bringin' things to a head," Rip said, squatting to remove the mustang's hobbles, "happens you gotta use them featherheads agin Stone Winslowe, and you figure he's gonna attack the keelboat at anchor, why not kill two birds with one piss squirt? Get the Comanches in on it. That'll guarantee a victory."

"It would," Fargo agreed. "And I considered it. But a Plains warrior is a big believer in giving the spoils to the victor."

"Ahuh, that shines."

"I gave my word to Mr. Majors," Fargo said, "that I'd scout those goods through to Wichita Falls, not barter them to Indians."

Fargo didn't add, however, that he just might have a perfect job for the Comanches. At the moment he was carefully studying the river valley below the headlands.

"No riders," he told Rip, "but we can't see the hidden ambushers."

"Should we skip the valley and ride on the tableland?"

Fargo shook his head. "You got it hindside foremost. There's cover in the valley. Let's ford the river and ride the Texas side—that's where the keelboat is, anyway. That way, if we're jumped by too many to fight, we'll take to the Texas plains and count on our horses to outrun 'em. Outlaw horses are sore-used and go puny in the long run."

Fargo tapped his heels and the Ovaro started down the steep face of the bluff, Rip a few yards behind.

"Don't be parading it," Fargo remarked casually, "but there's a Comanche spy watching us."

"Tender Virgin! Where?"

"Bottom of the bluff on our right. But don't be staring at him, old son. You know better than to let a red man see he's got you rattled."

"Damn it, Fargo, we're doin' the devil's own work, happens we ride with them Staked Plain marauders."

"Bottle it, Ranger Miller. I already gave my word."

"Your *word*?" Rip sputtered behind him. "To a damn renegade? What in pluperfect hell . . . ?"

"A man's word is his bond no matter who he gives it to."

They reached the verdant valley, and a few minutes later Fargo's pinto easily forded Red River. Both men kept a weather eye out, but there was no sign of white men or Comanches. There were no bluffs on this side of the river, and to the south a flat, endless horizon made it impossible for an enemy to sneak up on them.

"Plenty of bends in this river," Fargo told Rip. "I best hark to our backtrail. Just keep riding at a trot, and keep your eyes peeled."

Fargo wheeled the Ovaro and rode east for perhaps a mile, but

117

spotted neither fresh signs nor any men. He caught up with Rip again, and soon they were in sight of the keelboat. When they drew nearer, Etienne listlessly returned Fargo's greeting.

"If he looked any lower," Fargo remarked, "he'd be walking on his bottom lip."

Etienne rose from a log where he'd been seated near the water. The voyageurs who weren't on perimeter guard were scattered in small pockets, gambling with dice or betting on wrestling matches.

"Most ain't even totin' their rifles," Rip said scornfully. "Them town-bred sons of bitches couldn't pour pee out of a boot."

"You give them short measure," Fargo insisted. "When the fight actually commences, they'll stand and hold."

"Mebbe so. But I wouldn't give a plugged peso for the whole kit 'n' caboodle."

Both men swung down, Fargo shaking Etienne's hand before he and Rip tethered their mounts in the lush grass.

"Any trouble?" Fargo asked.

"*Beaucoup*. We are being watched by white men and Indians, Monsieur Fargo."

"Watched from where?"

"The Indians have not been here today, but they watch from the opposite bank. The white men come and go and watch us from the bluffs."

"Any of them fired on you?" Fargo asked.

Etienne shook his head. "So we have not fired at them. But my men . . . *Ciel!* They are close to mutiny."

"Been stall-fed too long," Rip insisted. "They've got soft."

"Pipe down, mouth," Fargo muttered. "They're in no mood to bear insults from an old gas pipe like you."

Fargo quickly filled the captain of voyageurs in on recent events upriver.

"This cannon," Etienne said when Fargo had finished, "where is it?"

"That's one nut I haven't cracked yet. But if you stay put, I doubt they'll drag it this far. They'll likely just scuttle the boat by knocking holes in the bottom."

Etienne caught his lower lip between his teeth. "An attack is coming soon, you say? The men have voted to turn the boat around and return downriver to Shreveport."

"That's more dangerous than staying," Fargo insisted. "That's right where Stone Winslowe wants them—on the water. Besides, they'll receive no wages, and the big bugs will never hire them again. Tell them they'll likely be killed to the last man if they try that. Their best choice is to stick and fight."

Reluctantly, Etienne nodded. Fargo unlashed the entrenching tool from behind his bedroll.

"Me and Rip are going to help you establish a reinforced position," Fargo explained. "A spot where all of us can take up positions behind siege defenses."

"Us?" Etienne repeated, hope sparking in his eyes. "*You* will fight beside us?"

"Hell, I'm part of this crew, ain't I? You think I'm going to stir up a hornet's nest and then run from the stings?"

Etienne shouted in French to his men. Whatever he said made some of them cheer, while others still looked sullen.

"Fargo," Rip said nervously, "are we really gonna stake our lives on these frog-talkin' city boys?"

"Why not? I've trusted a toothless old drunk so far, and I have no regrets. With good leadership, Rip, these boatmen will fight like Cheyenne Dog Soldiers."

Fargo turned to Etienne. "Before we build these defenses, tell me something—have you ever heard of Caswell Jones?"

Etienne made the Sign of the Cross. "The very devil! He is up on the Platte River, killing and plundering. He murders in— how you say?—*sang-froid*."

"You mean cold blood?"

Etienne nodded vigorously. "But he pays off the army officers handsomely, and they see no evil because they look for no evil."

"Well, maybe he's been on the Platte, but he'll be down on the Red River soon. He's due to meet up with Stone Winslowe and buy stolen goods."

At this intelligence, Etienne's copper skin lightened a few shades. "Monsieur Fargo, do you mean we must fight *both* men— and perhaps *peaux rouges* also? If I tell my crew they must fight Jones, *mon Dieu*! They will mutiny and kill me if I try to stop them."

"Don't get your bloomers in a bunch," Fargo calmed him. "If my plan works out, you and your men will be miles upriver when

119

Jones comes—and he'll never catch you. Now let's get this position prepared for battle."

Knowing that attackers would not ford, Fargo selected a good position at the top of the bank, with the river behind. For the next two hours, under Fargo's attentive supervision, the men dug two-man rifle pits and a protective ring of trip holes that were invisible in the deep grass. He put a detail to work cutting down saplings and sharpening both ends to make pointed stakes. These were pounded into the ground at a forty-five-degree slant and used to make a horseshoe-shaped siege defense around the rifle pits.

The general mood of the voyageurs improved as this work went forward. One man, however, argued hotly with Etienne.

"The hell they sayin'?" Rip asked Fargo. "I only palaver two languages: American and cussing."

"I can't decipher it either," Fargo admitted. "But it's obvious as a third tit that some of the men are dead-set against staying here."

"I'd shoot the high-handed bastard for mutiny. He'll give the rest chicken guts."

Fargo shook his head. "These ain't just hired jobbers—most of these men are related to Etienne by blood or marriage. Killing one *would* bring on a mutiny. He'll come around."

"Ahuh, well I ain't too keen on fightin' alongside these lily-livers."

Fargo fought back a sly grin. "I can't order you to, Rip. But having a Texas Ranger around to show these green troops how it's done would be a great help."

Rip, busy digging more trip holes with a shovel from the boat, puffed out his bony chest. "I reckon it would be, at that. Hell, I can't let these store-fed barbers' clerks die for want of a good battle captain."

"*Now* you're whistling," Fargo approved.

When the work was finished, Fargo visited the lazaret, the space set aside for ship's stores, and stocked up on hardtack, coffee, and dried fruit. He was halfway down the gangplank when a loud *thuck*, from a bullet impacting inches from his right foot, was followed by the crack of a rifle.

"Cover down!" he shouted, racing for the bank as more shots followed in rapid succession.

120

Fargo dived into a rifle pit, bullets whining all around him, and used the angle of impact to quickly trace the rounds back to their source: two men up on the bluffs on the Indian Territory side of the river, too far for handgun range. Seeing that Fargo carried no rifle, and obviously eager to kill him, they boldly sat their saddles.

Fargo leaped out of the pit, running a zigzag pattern, and headed for Rip's horse. He tugged the Spencer out of its saddle scabbard and took a position behind a gnarled cottonwood, Rip joining him. The ambushers apparently believed Fargo was still pinned down somewhere, and one used field glasses to spot him out.

Fargo settled the butt of the modified Spencer into his shoulder socket, took a long breath, relaxed his muscles, aimed plumb on the nearest man's torso, and slowly, steadily took up the trigger slack. The powerful weapon mule-kicked hard into his shoulder, and the huge slug literally blew the outlaw out of his saddle in a spray of blood and gobbets of flesh and organs.

The other would-be assassin fled for his life as a cheer erupted from the voyageurs.

"Done and *done!*" Rip said triumphantly. "That second bastard took off like a scalded dog."

"Incapacitated by fatigue through persistent retreating," Fargo quipped, quoting an army field report he'd once read.

By now the sun was a dull copper orb in the west, and soon the two men saddled up to leave for their cave.

"Monsieur Fargo," Etienne said quietly, "when do you think the attack will come?"

"Anytime now," he replied. "But we're camped between you and the outlaws, and they won't slip past us. You'll have some warning."

"Bonne chance!" Etienne called as they gigged their mounts forward.

"Thanks, we'll be needing it. And good luck to you, too."

Rip was in high spirits over the recent kill. He hardly paid attention when Fargo frowned, then pulled his binoculars out and studied the Texas plains to the south.

Eventually, however, Rip became aware of Fargo's grim face.

"The hell's biting at you, Trailsman?" he demanded. "You

121

just stoked the fighting fettle of them frogs, and here you are lookin' like the widow at a funeral."

"I saw a big dust puff to the south," Fargo replied. "It's about ten riders, all headed for the trading post. I'd say Stone Winslowe has called in reinforcements. We're up against it now, Rip."

15

Stone Winslowe did not drink liquor often, but when he did he could be an ugly drunk—a fact Belinda had discovered the hard way. He was drinking tonight, pouring it down like a pipe through the floor, and Belinda felt her stomach fist with nervous fear.

"Pour me another," he called out from the crude shakedown, "and not so much glass this time."

Stone looked agitated, his face drawn tight in worry lines, and Belinda knew that Skye Fargo was the author of his woes. She took the empty pony glass he handed her and filled it from a bottle of cheap wagon-yard whiskey sitting on the table.

Belinda always feared Stone, but tonight it was worse. There was a new, desperate recklessness in his manner that told her he had reached his Rubicon. Usually his eyes were small and dull like a turtle's, but right now they were intense, burning embers, and she wondered if she had seen her last sunrise.

She handed him the glass, hoping he wouldn't notice her trembling hands.

"Your hero ain't got a chance in hell, woman—know that? I know you're cheering him on, you brazen slut, but he's a gone-up case."

"I—I don't know what you mean, Stone," she stammered out.

"In a pig's ass, you don't! Fargo and Bradford are headed for a walking showdown, and Brad's got two dead brothers walking with him."

"This Fargo means nothing—"

"Shut your lying mouth. Brad ain't just quick—he's quicker than scat. You've seen him—he can draw on a man today and shoot him yesterday."

Stone took down half the whiskey in his glass in one gulp.

Even as he was speaking, gunshots could be heard behind the building, unrelenting.

"Hear that?" he continued, those apocalyptic eyes boring into her. "That's Brad practicing—not that he needs it. He's like a man possessed. You might think he ain't got any 'brotherly love' in him, but Fargo stepped on a snake when he killed Clint and Bo."

He fell into a brooding silence, still watching her. His eyes had grown speculative. "You know something?" he said in a calm, quiet voice that made her heart stomp against her ribs.

"What, Stone?"

"You know how, sometimes, you notice something, but don't get it until later?"

He knows, an inner voice screamed at her. But she remained calm on the surface. "Yes, I think I know what you mean."

"Like a couple days back," he went on. "You went out for a long bath," he went on. "But your hair was dry when you came in. How's come?"

Blood rushed into her face, heating it, and she hoped he didn't notice in the candlelight.

"Sometimes," she replied, trying to keep her voice casual, "I bathe everything but my hair—it takes so long to dry and drips on everything."

The rage was on him instantly. The veins in his neck bulged out fat as night crawlers. He threw his glass into a wall, shattering it, and leaped out of the bed. He slapped her so hard, it jolted her down to her feet.

"Talk out, damn you! Admit you're a lying whore, woman! That Fargo's got him a reputation for bulling women, and I think he bulled *you*."

"No, Stone, that's *not* true! You're thinking all of this only because he looked at me too long, as many men have done. I don't even like his type—he's a dusty saddle tramp, so poor he has to wear buckskins like some wild savage. His kind sleeps on the ground every night, no better off than a wild animal. No decent woman could long for a man like that."

Her lie was born of desperation, but it seemed to have some calming effect. Stone didn't really believe her, but he seemed less cocksure. He picked the bottle up from the table and took a long swig.

"Well, that makes some sense," he told her, "and maybe I'm wrong about him topping you. But still, I know what you hope—you hope the buckskin hero's gonna save you and your kin. But you're as wrong as wrong can be. I've lost two brothers to that crusading son of a bitch, and I got a sweet operation going along this river. I'm in it to win it."

His speech was starting to slur. He took another swig and staggered back to the bed. "Sure," he admitted, "for the past week or so Fargo has been my hair shirt. But I got men up from deep Texas, hard killers all. Brad's going to throw down on him, and Fargo won't realize it until his guts catch on fire. You can chisel it in granite, missy."

Now his manner changed once again as hungry eyes pored over her length. "Strip," he ordered her. "You know what to do."

Dread and nausea filled her like a bucket under a tap, but his mercurial temper frightened her. She unbuttoned her dress and let it fall to the floor, then shucked off her chemise and petticoat. She could hear his breath whistling in his nostrils when she tugged off her frilly pantaloons and stood naked.

Belinda reached up to free her hair, which was neatly coiled under a tortoiseshell comb.

"Don't touch it," he snapped. "This way you look like a schoolteacher."

This was the part she always feared—when he failed to get hard and then blew up, blaming her. She rubbed her body with both hands, cupping her breasts as if offering them to him.

"Am I helping you, Stone?" she asked, almost wishing he *would* get hard and end all this humiliation.

"Not so's you'd notice," he replied sarcastically. He handed her a feather he plucked from his pillow. "Do like I showed you—make 'em stiff."

Her face flushed with more shame, she tickled her nipples until they hardened. Stone finally cursed in frustration.

"It's you, not me," he snarled. "Cold and hoity-toity . . . you *do* know how to dampen a man's fire, don't you? I'll bet you piss icicles."

Hope surged through her when she realized the whiskey had made him sleepy. His eyelids drooped, and his next remark was mostly mumbled.

"Whore, that's what you are—a sparkling doxie. I'm getting you one of them lamps with a red shade . . . maybe line the boys up at a dollar a whack . . ."

His breathing went deep and even. She knew from experience that her "husband" was a deep sleeper, especially when drunk. Belinda quickly dressed and moved to the thin partition that divided the crude living quarters from the fake trading post. The slab door's leather hinges creaked only slightly when she pushed it open.

The room had no windows and she groped her way carefully toward the long deal counter at the other end. On the night that Fargo had burned down the saloons, he had also killed at least one man, and one of the outlaws had brought the dead man's gun belt here, leaving it on the counter. None of the Winslowe brothers seemed to notice it, and she had hidden it behind the counter under an old horse blanket.

But it could be too easily discovered there, and Belinda wanted it for herself—especially now that these hard-eyed men from Texas had entered the picture. She had faith in Skye Fargo, but no man could be expected to beat odds that included Bradford Stone. The prisoners would be killed and so would she after she was raped by every man here.

Belinda had different plans—if her fear became reality, with this gun she would kill that vulgar brute Stone Winslowe, then turn it on herself. While the pale moon inched toward its zenith, and her fancy coined these disturbing ideas, she nudged open a door in the rear of the trading post and cautiously studied the moonlit vista.

The gunshots had ceased some time ago, and she could see no one out back within the walled compound. She hurried to a wooden water trough and tucked the rolled-up gun belt underneath it. Belinda was rounding the old freight wagon when, abruptly, she almost ran smack into Bradford Winslowe.

"Oh! My stars, Bradford, you frightened the daylights out of me."

"Except it *ain't* daylight, is it?" With a grip tight as a vise, he grabbed her arm. "The hell you doing out here, girl?"

"Why . . . I just came outside for a . . . necessary trip."

"Hell, you got a slop pail inside, ain't you?"

"Yes, but I prefer to go outside."

The grip on her arm tightened. "Sure you do. Stone says you been meetin' Fargo outside, letting him put your ankles behind your ears. You just his whore, or are you also his spy?"

In the silver-white moon glow, his hard, tight-lipped mouth was straight as a seam. Only his eyes grinned—malevolently. She had to admit he looked cruelly handsome.

"Stone is jealous," she said bluntly. "He saw this man Fargo ogle me one time, and now imagination's loom is weaving all sorts of stories."

"I can't blame Stone. This moonlight makes that skin of yours glow like pearl. Makes me want to see the rest of you. Your loss, though, Little Miss Pink Cheeks—I'll eat off any other man's plate, but not my brother's."

Handsome or not, in the moonlight he looked like a madman. When he drew his six-gun and cocked it, her heart leaped into her throat.

"Just in case you *are* planning to meet that cock-chafer Fargo, girl, you best know this—this whole area is lousy with guards. I'm *watching* you, blondie, and if I find out you're spreading your legs for the man who killed Bo and Clint, I'll shoot you to streamers—*after* I get my use of you."

He let go of her arm, and she hurried back to the trading post. She was still a few feet from the door when the sound of his gun, and a sharp tug in her hair, caused a little cry from her. Her tortoiseshell comb shattered into tiny pieces, and her neatly coiled hair slid down in a heavy mass. She heard his mocking, arrogant laugh behind her.

"Better warn your buckskin boy what kind of shooting he's up against," Bradford chided her. "Tell him the Angel of Death is coming—coming real soon now!"

The sun had risen two hours earlier and now sent streaks of light dancing on the fast current of Red River. Fargo and Rip had taken up hidden positions, just outside the cave, that allowed them an excellent view of the valley and the plains to the south. By climbing to the pinnacle of the sandstone tumble, Fargo could also monitor the plains of the Indian Territory to the north.

"Nothing much stirring north of us," he reported as he climbed down from the pinnacle, "except a herd of antelope and a stray buff or two. See anything on your side?"

Rip didn't seem to hear him. His rheumy, tired eyes just gazed toward the river as if mesmerized.

Fargo raised his voice. "Rip! What's on your mind besides your hat?"

The old roadster flinched. "Sorry, Fargo. It's just . . . since talkin' to Justin the night he was killed, it's come home to me hard what a fix them hostages is in."

"They're in one world of hurt," Fargo agreed.

"One damn meal a day, and Mrs. Halfpenny bad sick. You must be frettin' about that pretty heifer, huh?"

"About *all* of them," Fargo corrected him. "They're just simple pilgrims who took a wrong turn into hell. Belinda's little brother is just a sprout. What makes it worse, I don't dare risk going back to that outlaw hellhole now. There's so many riders out, I can't even scout the upcountry of the river."

"You'd have to be soft between the head handles to try it," Rip agreed.

"Far as what happened to Justin," Fargo went on, "I never should've called him out beyond the gate."

Rip shook his head. "Sheep dip. There was no other way, and you needed to talk to him."

"Oh, I ain't tearing my hair out over it. But I knew it was dicey, so I can't claim innocence. And I sure don't look forward to telling Rebecca Halfpenny exactly how her husband was rubbed out."

Rip grunted. "Huh. Howsomever that may be, Fargo, ain't nobody took more risks in this deal than you. You ain't no halfway man, that's a fact. Boy, you got enough guts to fill a smokehouse, and you can look that woman straight in the eye—happens them bastards don't kill her and the rest."

"Those Comanche renegades don't do things halfway, either," Fargo said, pointing toward the river with his chin. "That spy keeps getting closer and closer, reminding us."

Rip scowled. "Ahuh, remindin' us it's comin' down to the nut cuttin'. Happens you plan to keep your word to them, best do it quick before we end up hangin' from hooks in our tits."

Fargo nodded. "Yeah, soon. My plan is still sorta scratched out in the dirt."

The Comanche rode up into the bluffs, his mission accomplished. Fargo fell into a muse, his face grim.

"You stewin' on Bradford?" Rip asked. "He talks the he-bear talk, but unless he ropes you into a draw-shoot, he'll show the white feather."

"Oh, I'll settle his hash," Fargo predicted confidently. "But those Winslowe brothers are just the vanguard, Rip. First the buffalo will be exterminated, then the Indians. We can kill all four Winslowes, but thousands will come behind them."

"Ahuh. Too many men see nothin' but money out here."

"Amen, brother," Fargo agreed. "Thanks to the howlers and katydid boosters, the frontier won't stand a chance."

"Won't go to hell in my lifetime," Rip predicted. "You'll have to swallow more of it, so you might's well get used to it."

Fargo shook his head. "I'd sooner get used to cholera. Right now the sod-house frontier is still peaceful. But soon enough all the scratch-penny herds of cattle will grow into that beef bonanza you mentioned, and the land will be fenced and posted against trespassing. Soon enough the dirt scratchers will be warring with the cattle kings. Then the miners and timber cutters will pitch into the game. It won't end until they've ruined the West."

Rip chuckled. "Yessir, you're no halfway man, Fargo. To hear you take on about it, anyplace with board sidewalks is too civilized."

Fargo grinned, eyes sweeping the river country below. "I don't go that far, old son. I like a card game and a shot of whiskey now and again, and I appreciate a hotel bed."

"My old pap made me read the Bible when I was a tad," Rip said. "Accordin' to the Good Book, God gave men 'dominion' over all He made. Don't that mean we can do whatever we want to with the land?"

"I'm not Bible raised," Fargo admitted. "But why would God bother creating such beautiful land and not care at all how it was treated?"

Rip pulled at his chin. "That's a poser, all right."

Fargo lifted his field glasses to peer through them. "Here's another one. What is an Apache tracker doing this far north?"

"An Apache? Boy, are you sure?"

"Would a cow lick Lot's wife? Sheepskin pad for a saddle, red headband, wearing high-topped moccasins . . . that's an Apache, all right."

"Hell, they never even put their mark on the Fort Laramie

treaty," Rip said, still incredulous. "They got no legal right to be in The Nations. Last I heard, they was way down south in the Dragoon Mountains, raiding into Mexico. The Governor of Chihuahua is paying a two-hunnert-peso bounty for each Apache scalp."

"Yeah," Fargo said, still studying the tracker as he moved beside the river in fits and starts. "But I think I know what's going on here. Stone Winslowe is taking a leaf from my own book."

Rip followed the Apache's progress with his naked eyes. "You mean, that bunch from Texas brought him up with them yesterday?"

"Sure. Outlaws possess lousy trailcraft. Well, I'll be damn . . ."

Fargo focused his binoculars. He studied the deeply weathered, careworn face that reflected the hard environment of the sterile deserts in the New Mexico Territory and northern Mexico. "Hell, I know him. Jemez. He's an Apache turncoat who works for the army sometimes. We scouted together on the Jornada."

"Fargo, is there a red Arab you *don't* know? Lemme have a squint."

Rip studied the tracker through Fargo's glasses. "Christ, he looks like a hard winter. Is them *Apache* scalps on his sash?"

"Yep. Prob'ly means to swap them to somebody who can collect the bounty. The Apaches ain't sentimental about tribal loyalties and such."

When the Apache was within hailing distance, Fargo stepped into view. "Jemez! *Ven aqui!* Come here! It's Fargo!"

The Apache raised one hand high in the sign of peaceful intentions and slapped his painted mustang's rump.

"Can you palaver in Mexer talk?" Rip asked.

"Some. Apaches know a little Spanish and English, so I mix it up."

Rip said, "Stone wants us out of the way. I'd wager he's all set to attack that keelboat."

"Tomorrow. Maybe even today," Fargo agreed. "And those Texas outlaws have experience fighting Mexican soldiers and bandits. Stone's original crew are mostly highwaymen and smugglers—they run from a hard fight. But this new bunch are hard-tempered killers, and we won't run them off. They'll have to be popped over."

By now Jemez had ridden most of the way up the bluff. The last slope was steep and he dismounted, leading his pony by the horsehair bridle. An old rifle musket was lashed to his saddle, but the only weapon on his person was a curved skinning knife.

"Nantan Fargo," he called out in greeting, using the title Apaches used as a mark of respect toward certain white men. "Many sleeps, uh?"

"Been a while," Fargo agreed. "Still work for the army?"

"No work. Got hungry, ate a *mula*. Major make me *paga cuarenta dolares*. No more damn army."

Fargo grinned. "He ate an army mule," he told Rip. "Had to pay forty dollars."

He looked at Jemez again. "So now you're hired to track me down?"

Jemez nodded. "*Al principio*, at first, I do not know who I track. *Entonces*, then, up here, Stone say look for man *con caballo magnifico*, fine black-and-white pinto. *Entonces*, I know it is Nantan Fargo."

Fargo avoided using the Apache's name again, knowing his tribe feared their names lost their power if spoken before whites. "Let me guess," he said. "You were given half your money to lure you up here."

Jemez grinned and pulled a chamois sack from his parfleche. "*Veinte dolares de plato*. Twenty silver dollars."

"And you will get the other half when you tell Stone *donde yo estoy*, where I am?"

Jemez nodded. "*Yo no soy necio*, I am no fool. He means to *matame*, kill me, if I go back. I will leave now after I say hello to Nantan Fargo, *mi amigo*. There are Comanches in this place, they will roast me."

"Wait," Fargo said. He went into the cave and returned with hardtack, jerky, and fruit for Jemez's long journey.

Jemez smiled and nodded. It was the Indian custom to always give something in return for a gift. He pulled a round, smooth stone from his parfleche.

"Always keep this on you," he told Fargo. "This will make it difficult *por sus enemigos*, for your enemies, to find your tracks."

Without any ceremony, or good-byes, the Apache leaped onto

131

his horse. Both men watched him descend the bluff, ford Red River, and bear south across the Texas plains.

"Fargo," Rip said, "I'd never call you an Indian lover. But I'm powerful glad you know their ways."

"Apple polishing is wasted on me, old son."

"No, I'm serious as a gut shot. Mebbe if us Rangers woulda learned somethin' about 'em, besides just how to kill 'em, more of us would still be above the horizon."

"Maybe," Fargo said. "But the white man's stick floats one way, the red man's the other. Niles Wolcott is a good man, and his peaceful ways up at the Lone Grove agency might work with Cherokees. But tribes like the Apaches and Comanches are killers. If Jemez had felt safe, he would have turned our location in to Stone Winslowe."

"Yet you're *still* willing to trust Comanches?"

Fargo grinned. "Trust everybody but cut the cards. We got one hell of a battle coming up, Rip, so we'll have to roll the dice. The bad news is, they might kill us."

"Ahuh, so what's the good news?"

"Comanches aren't cannibals—they won't likely eat us."

•

16

Fargo and Rip remained vigilant for the rest of the day, watching north and south of Red River, but no attack party rode out from the trading post.

"Prob'ly waiting to hear from Jemez," Fargo speculated as the two men made a meager supper of stale hardtack and dried fruit.

"Comin' on to dark now," Rip said, poking at the fire with a stick. "Think they'll mount a nighttime raid?"

Fargo shook his head. "Not under a half-moon and a cloudy sky. They know, from their spies, there'll be resistance, and that means they have to have clear targets."

"Tomorrow at sunrise?"

"That might depend on how close Caswell Jones is," Fargo replied. "I suggest we tack up and find out what's on the spit downriver."

Rip emitted a weary grunt as he rose from the cave floor, kneecaps popping. "Now I see why they call you the Trailsman— you live in the saddle. Well, happens a man wants his life over quick, just ride with Skye Fargo."

"I have pushed you hard, old campaigner," Fargo said. "Hell, I'm worn out down to the marrow myself. You're welcome to sit this one out."

"What, and get my pizzle cut off by Comanches? Let's make tracks."

Preferring to avoid the easy, but well-patrolled, river route, they stuck to the bluffs as they rode east. The rough trail was sandy and rocky, with washouts that had to be detoured. A rising moon lighted the very tips of the bluffs like silver patina, but rock-shelf overhangs continually plunged them into darkness.

Fearful of injuring the Ovaro in the shadowy terrain, Fargo held him to a trot.

"Here's a good one," Rip said. "This boy named Harry Dix was known as a troublemaker at school, right? So one day, at lunch, him and a few other boys climb atop the school and commence to tossin' dirt clods at the other kids.

"One a them clods hits the teacher smack in the ass. She looks up and sees the boys. 'All right!' she hollers out. 'All you boys up there with Harry Dix get down here right now!' And one o' the boys yells back, 'If we only got peach fuzz, can we stay up here?'"

Fargo groaned like a soul in torment. "They banned that old relic on the *Mayflower*. C'mon, let's head down to the river—I think we're past any night riders now."

Earlier in the evening huge blowflies had tormented men and horses. Now, as the night advanced and they eased down the face of the bluff, inch-long mosquitoes replaced the flies.

"All these ducks and geese and quail I seen earlier," Rip complained, "and us eatin' rabbit. I seen a deer, too. I wouldn't mind getting outside of some decent grub."

Fargo ignored him realizing they were closing in on Etienne and his crew.

"Let's ki-yi our mounts," he called to Rip, hammering the Ovaro's ribs with his heels. The pinto's ears flattened back, and his stride lengthened.

"It's Fargo and Rip coming in!" he shouted, spotting a campfire. "Hold your powder, men!"

Fargo tore around the siege defenses, aiming for the fire at river's edge. At the last moment he reined back hard, the Ovaro's skidding forelegs scattering dirt and grass on a surprised Etienne.

"Sorry 'bout that," Fargo said. "I wanted to be a hard target in case your men got trigger happy."

"The attack is coming?" Etienne asked, his voice tight with nervousness.

"Not tonight. I predict tomorrow just after sunrise. I'm heading downriver now to look for Caswell Jones. I'll stop here again on my way back."

Fargo noticed it was unnaturally quiet in the usually raucous riverside camp, each man alive with his thoughts as the battle loomed.

He remained in the saddle. "Etienne, take these last instructions to all your men. No prisoners, no survivors. Kill them to the last man—*no* mercy, understood?"

Etienne nodded in the ruby-tinted firelight. "No mercy."

"Also tell your men: in the heat of battle, just shoot to hit. But when down to their last cartridges, shoot for head or heart. And if they start to overrun you, shoot the damn horses first. Then shoot the riders before they can get up. All clear?"

"*Mais oui*, Monsieur Fargo."

"Good man. See you later tonight."

Staying back from the river, Fargo kicked the Ovaro up to an easy lope, a pace he rarely used after dark. In places the lush grass grew so tall it shined their boots as they rode through it. Fargo kept his eyes on the moonlit river.

They had ridden perhaps fifteen miles, just past the trading post at Colbert, when Fargo spotted several fires straight ahead. He reined in.

"Rip, I'd wager that's Caswell Jones and his scurvy-ridden crew. Let's hook to the right and get behind cover. Then we'll walk our horses in. Get that thumb-buster of yours ready," Fargo added, meaning the dragoon pistol.

Ten minutes later they were sheltered behind wild plum bushes with a good view of the well-lighted camp and a huge keelboat anchored beyond it. Since Fargo and Rip only required a look-see, and might need a fast getaway, both men held their horses by the bridles.

Fargo's eye was immediately drawn to a boatman who stood out like a rhinestone vest, a huge bear of a man, strong as horse-radish, blunt, and bull-necked with shoulders broad as a yoke. He ignored the drunken riot all around him, crimping a cigarette paper and shaking some tobacco into it.

"Meet Caswell Jones," Fargo whispered. "Talk about your sneer of cold command."

"Ahuh. You could toss him in a pond and skim ugly for a month. I'll bet that son of a bitch would steal dead flies from blind spiders. *All* these skunk-bit coyotes would."

It was difficult, with so many men shifting about, for Fargo to get a fair estimate of their numbers, but he put them at twenty or so. A few men stood buck naked, boiling their clothes in a giant kettle to kill lice and other vermin. They shared a bottle as they stirred their clothing with an oar.

What sounded like a gunshot made both intruders flinch. Then Fargo spotted a drunk boatman seated near a fire, tossing bullets into the flames and giggling like a madman.

"Man, he's got a skinful," Fargo said.

"Jesus! Look just left of him, Fargo."

When Fargo realized what he was watching, he felt his gorge rise. The men had evidently kidnapped two Caddo Indian girls—a tribe of north Texas—and were taking turns raping them. Even as Fargo watched, lips curling back from his teeth in rage, the last man in line shot both of them in the head.

"Let's get the hell out of here," he whispered to Rip. "This bunch reminds me of the scalpers I fought down in Mexico."

Fargo turned the stirrup, swung up and over, then yanked the Ovaro around to the west. Their luck had been good all night, but suddenly the wheel of fortune took a downward plunge.

Rip had just inserted his foot in the stirrup and started to heave himself up when the angry buzzing of a rattlesnake spooked his mustang. The scrub reared almost straight up, flinging Rip backward hard. His cocked dragoon hit the ground and fired, startling the river camp into ominous silence.

An eyeblink later, however, a dozen weapons opened up, and bullets shredded the plum bushes. Fargo wanted only to flee, knowing Jones' men had no mounts on which to pursue, nor could he afford to use much of his ammo, wanting to conserve it for the coming battle with Stone Winslowe's hired army. But Rip needed time to calm his horse, and already those drunken-brave boatmen were closing in on them.

Luckily, the modified Spencer, too, had fallen from Rip's saddle scabbard. Fargo leaped down, threw the Ovaro's reins forward to hold him, then scooped up the rifle. He took an off-hand-kneeling position and sought a target.

"I see these boys are feeling sparky," he muttered.

The same man who had murdered the Caddo women was advancing recklessly—but he made the mistake of letting the biggest fire backlight him, and Fargo literally blew him off his feet.

That slowed the charge, but some men didn't see their comrade's torso explode. Fargo picked another man, and this time he shot for the groin. The man's hideous screams of pain acted as a brake on the other men's initiative—some ran for the boat while others cowered in the tall grass. Several kept firing, a few of the bullets almost finding their mark.

"Got him!" Rip said, finally forking leather. "Fargo, for Christ sakes, let's get out of the weather!"

Fargo, Rip, and Etienne huddled near one of the fires.

"I gave you my word, Etienne, and I meant it," Fargo said. "It's true that Jones is not far downriver, but I guarantee you'll never see him again. Not alive, anyway."

Rip, who had guessed Fargo's plan by now, looked skeptical. But he wisely kept his opinion to himself.

"How far downriver?" the captain of voyageurs pressed.

"Just a whoop and a holler from here," Fargo admitted. "I'd say fifteen miles. But don't worry—they'll never get this far."

Etienne slowly nodded acceptance. "And Stone Winslowe? You are sure he will attack tomorrow?"

"Affirmative. Remember, he's in touch with Jones and almost surely knows where that boat is. Now, Jones is about forty miles from Stone's outpost. Going against this strong current, even using sails and poles, it would take at least two days, maybe three, for Jones to get there—and I say he's *never* going to get there. But Winslowe doesn't know that, and he'll want to be ready with the goods he plans to steal from our boat. So the attack will commence tomorrow."

Etienne nodded. "We will be ready. You will camp here tonight?"

"No," Fargo said. "Rip and me are going to be roving skirmishers, see how many we can kill from their flanks while Stone's bunch is on its way. When they arrive, we'll be salting their tails."

Fargo stood up. "Etienne, there's a big coil of towing rope belowdecks. I want you to cut me off a piece big enough to span the river with about twenty feet extra. I'm gonna make a little ride back downriver to a spot I picked out earlier."

The moment the Creole had hurried off, Rip said, "That Etienne is a plumb good sort, Fargo. The man puts a lot of trust in you, and hell, so do I. But this 'plan' you got for dealin' with Jones is mostly air pudding."

"It's a gamble," Fargo admitted, his voice cheerful. "But I'm an old hand at stacking the deck. Why'n'cha roll up in your blanket and catch a few winks? I'll be back in a shake."

Finally back at Rip's cave, a weary and sleepy Fargo stripped the leather from his stallion, then rubbed him down before feeding him parched corn from his hat.

"Fargo, I won't swallow your bunk like Etienne will," Rip said. "Comanches won't attack a boat that big and well armed."

"They will when I explain this good deal to them and the help I'm giving them."

"Christ, you had ten—"

"Ten Cherokee policemen offered to me, I know," Fargo cut him off. "Set it to music, old man. So maybe I screwed the pooch. You like to forget that *I* didn't invite the Comanches— they invited themselves. Do you want to tell Comanche renegades to kiss your white ass?"

Rip poked at the fire. "Naw. You're right. A man bends with the breeze or he breaks."

"Sing it, brother. And right now the breeze is Comanche, not Cherokee."

Fargo squatted at the fire for several minutes, turning this problem back and forth for a while, studying all of its facets. Finally he sighed and stood up.

"I got no choice," he said to no one in particular.

Fargo walked out front, fired two shots in the air, then returned to the fire. Fifteen minutes later, Medicine Flute, the brave who surprised him days earlier in the cave, appeared in the firelight.

"The time has come, Son of Light?"

"The time has come." Fargo pointed to a space between himself and Rip at the fire. "Come sit, Medicine Flute, and I will speak words you can place in your parfleche."

17

The sun broke over the eastern flats, revealing fog on the river bluffs, a shifting blanket of pure white cotton. Fargo and Rip sat out front of the well-hidden cave, drinking their second cup of strong black coffee—"strong enough to float a horseshoe," as Rip had bragged when he brewed it.

"Hope that damn fog burns off quick-like," Rip groused. "It's clear down below on the tableland, but we can't hardly see it from here."

"Sun's already hot," Fargo pointed out. "This will burn off fast. Besides, I've never known of outlaws to be disciplined. They'll be late riding out."

"T'hell with discipline, I don't like the odds. Countin' Etienne, they's thirteen voyageurs. With us, that makes fifteen men agin mebbe twenty-five outlaws."

Fargo laughed. "This from a Texas Ranger."

"Texas Rangers is good shots. You yourself admit them frogs can't hit a tent from the inside. Hell, they might even break and run."

"They won't back down. Run where—into the river? Besides, scratch a boatman and you'll find a brawler."

"That's fistfights. Can they stand up to lead?"

"You give up too quick, old son. Those Creoles stand a good chance. They're dug in deeper than ticks on a hound and surrounded by siege defenses."

Fargo thought he detected movement to the west. He lifted his brass-framed field glasses and studied the purpled shadows.

"Here they come," he announced. "Riding single file on the Texas side of the river."

"How many?" Rip demanded.

"Can't tell yet. But plenty, all totin' rifles and scatterguns."

"God's gumdrops! Our hash is cooked."

Fargo felt a sting of irritation and lowered his glasses, staring at the other man. "Swallow your gizzard. Rip, you been a strong right arm to me so far, but damn, are you a nervous Nellie all of a sudden. Maybe you best reach down inside your trousers and see if you got a set on you."

Rip's creased face collapsed into a mask of shame. "I got a confession to make, Fargo. I told you some stretchers. I did work for the Texas Rangers, but I never rode with 'em. See, I was a cook at the Ranger barracks on the Brazos River."

Fargo laughed. "Hell, every man out west tells some stretchers. I once had a little redhead believing I stole a steamboat."

"She fell for that?"

"Sure," Fargo said, "until I told her I came back for the river."

"I did know Captain Coleman," Rip hastened to add. "He even taught me, the horse wrangler, and the messenger rider how to shoot on account there was Comanche attacks at the barracks."

"Look, I never believed you were a Ranger," Fargo admitted. "You made too many mistakes. But you're a good pard. You want to stay in the cave today?"

"Hell no. I come this far, and I mean to see it through."

"Good man," Fargo said. "Just nerve up. I predict this is gonna be a coffee-cooling detail."

Fargo believed no such thing, but it was his habit to stay cheerful before a hard fight. By now the line of outlaws was almost even with their position.

"Look at 'em," Rip muttered. "Spurring their horses in the shoulders. Them bastards think a horse is just a cheap tool."

"Why wouldn't they? Most likely, they're all stolen."

"You were right," Rip said. "The fog's burned off."

Fargo nodded. "Notice how Stone and Bradford are riding as flankers," he said. "That puts them out of range of the bored-out Spencer gun. Bet you a dollar to a doughnut they didn't tell this Texas bunch about it."

"Hell," Rip said, "how'd Stone get them Texicans to ride for him?"

"How else? Money is like manure—it works best when you spread it around."

"Ahuh. Well, back in the States they'd all be boosted branch-

140

ward for a play like this. But in The Nations, they can murder and plunder openly."

"That's why," Fargo said, heading back into the cave, "now and then 'law' has to appoint itself."

He returned carrying the special killing rifle.

Rip grinned. "Time for these jaspers to meet the widow-maker, huh?"

"Why not? I like to come right out of the chute bucking. After last night's fandango against Caswell Jones and his crew, we've got eight rounds left. I promised Medicine Flute to save at least two. That leaves six rounds to thin these sons of bitches out right now."

Rip gauged the distance and frowned. "Six? Hell, Fargo, they must be six or seven hundred yards out. I figure you might get one or two before the rest ride out of range."

Fargo took up a prone position, making a little hollow in the dirt for his left elbow. "Rip, the cartridges for my Henry pack a two-hundred-grain powder load. I don't know the caliber of these rounds, but judging from the recoil and the target damage, I'd say they pack at least six hundred grains. We'll soon find out how far it can score hits."

Fargo pulled down his hat against the swirling dust, levered a round into the chamber, and secured the butt plate into his shoulder. Since Stone and Bradford were harder targets, he settled the crosshairs of the scope on the head of the first rider in line. *Slow and steady*, he told himself as he took up the trigger slack, exhaling evenly to avoid bucking the gun.

The powerful cartridge detonated and the Spencer kicked hard into his shoulder. The outlaw's head exploded like a melon under a sledgehammer.

"Score!" Rip exclaimed. "But there they go, Fargo, turning south!"

The riders jerked rein and sank steel into their mounts, but it wasn't easy to outrun triple-loaded bullets and a telescopic sight. Fargo levered quickly, dropped the hairs on a retreating outlaw, and wiped him out of the saddle.

"Score!" Rip shouted again.

Fargo levered, sighted, hit a third man dead center.

"Score, by Christ! *Go* it, Fargo!"

Fargo tagged a fourth rider, hitting a little high but blowing a fist-sized hole through his neck.

"Two more, Fargo, and you got your six!" Rip spurred him on.

As Fargo selected his fifth target, however, he spotted danger. A man with a Sharps Big Fifty, a dangerous gun out to eight hundred yards, lay in the grass aiming toward them.

"Cover down!" he called to Rip. "Buff gun!"

The wind-bent grass made it difficult to find a good bead on the outlaw. Through his sights Fargo watched the man lower the breach block and insert a long cartridge into the chamber. Fargo squeezed off his fifth round and blew a hole in the owlhoot's chest, blood spuming in arcing gouts. Fargo noticed, grinning with satisfaction, that no one dared to pick up the dangerous weapon.

By now the rest had retreated south too far, and Fargo had to settle for five kills instead of six.

"Great day in the morning!" Rip exalted. "That's one humdinger of a rifle, Fargo. And you're one hell of a shootist."

"I reckon that took some of the vinegar out of 'em," Fargo allowed modestly.

Rip loosed a yawp of triumph. "Boy, you shot the piewaddin' out of 'em. I wonder how Stone and Bradford like *them* apples—Clint's rifle, I mean, bein' used agin 'em."

"Settle down. This is no time to recite our coups. Let's hit leather and get behind these old boys. The killing's just beginning, Rip, and the rest won't be this easy."

Fargo always favored the simplest battle tactics, and the job of roving skirmishers was to thin out a body of attackers before they closed with the defenders. He had gotten off to a good start with the five kills from the bluffs, but he still didn't like the odds. Outlaws were used to facing flying lead, but Etienne and his crew were not.

Fargo and Rip rode down the bluff and forded the Red, Fargo vigilant for any rearguard force.

"No point in wasting these weapons," he told Rip as they rode past the five dead men. "But hauling too many into battle will just get in our way. Grab a six-shooter and a scattergun."

Fargo selected a double-ten express gun, barrel sawed off to ten inches, and shoved a Volcanic repeater into his gun belt. The

142

handgun was only .32 caliber, but known to be accurate and reliable. Rip picked up a 12-gauge Greener and a Colt Navy.

"Let's raise dust," Fargo said. "They've got a good jump on us. But keep your eyes to all sides—they might've left ambushers behind."

Both riders urged their mounts to a fast lope. Thanks to the serpentine twisting of the river, the outlaws remained out of sight ahead. But Fargo saw a scaled quail suddenly whir out from a clump of hawthorn bushes about a hundred feet in front of them.

He reined in and caught Rip's eye, pointing at the bushes. "Hold my horse," he muttered, tossing Rip the reins and swinging down.

Fargo drew and thumb-cocked his Colt, went straight down to the riverbank, then crept up behind the bushes. He spotted the rumps of two horses and, just past the mounts, two hardcases armed with rifles.

"You fellows got a match?" Fargo called out.

Both men started and spun around. Fargo's first shot drilled the one on the left straight through the heart, but his luck ran out with the next shot. Factory ammo of that day was notoriously unreliable, and Fargo's second bullet was a hangfire. This was all the time the second outlaw required to open fire with a long Jennings rifle.

A bullet passed so close that Fargo felt the wind-rip on his neck. He got his single-action Colt cocked, but the Jennings was spitting fire and lead, and he was forced to dive headlong into brush.

"Eat *this*, you crusading bastard!" the outlaw snarled, sensing victory and closing in on Fargo.

The Trailsman snapped off a shot blind, brush blocking his face, but the rounds came snapping in, one tugging his shirt as it penetrated a sleeve.

An eyeblink later, Rip's confiscated Greener roared from the other side of the brush. A stray pellet smacked into Fargo's ass, stinging like a snakebite, but most of the load turned the owl-hoot's beard-scruffed face into chopped meat, and he crumpled to the grass, screaming like a scalped man.

Fargo climbed out and tossed a finishing shot into him. "Nice work, Rip," he called out. "You just saved my bacon—at least, the part you didn't shoot."

Fargo took a minute to strip the leather from both outlaw horses and remove their hobbles. They'd have plenty of graze and water in this area, and might take up with a herd of wild horses. Then the two horsebackers picked up the trail of the attacking outlaws, Fargo wincing as he bounced in the saddle.

"That's seven down," he called over to Rip. "You're some pumpkins with a shotgun."

"I just took a guess and hoped to hell you was hunkered down."

Ten minutes later they rode out of a dogleg bend and saw the tail end of Stone Winslowe's attacking force.

"Shit-oh-dear," Fargo said when the last rider slued around to look back. He recognized the low-crowned hat with its sharply curled brim. "That's Bradford—wheel and retreat! We're in his range."

Fargo's Henry was sheathed, and he couldn't get it at the ready fast enough, and the express gun was worthless at this range. So was a handgun to anybody but a trick shot like Winslowe. Since Fargo never pushed if a thing wouldn't move, retreat was the best option.

Just to buy time for Rip and throw off Winslowe's concentration, Fargo jerked the Volcanic from his gun belt and snapped off three quick rounds before he faded back.

His ploy might have worked. Bradford missed with six rounds, although one nicked Fargo's left stirrup.

"Christ, I hope he don't charge us," Rip fretted.

"Ah, he won't. He's got sand in a draw-shoot only because he knows he can't lose. But taking his chances on a galloping horse requires *cojones* he ain't got. He's all gurgle and no guts."

The keelboat camp lay just ahead, and Fargo heard the opening volleys from both sides.

"Let's close with 'em," Fargo told Rip. "We'll split up when we get there. But for Christ sakes, *don't* lose sight of Bradford or he'll snuff your wick. Stay behind the trees, stay in motion, and pick off as many as you can."

Both men kicked their mounts forward. They cleared a line of jack pines and found a ferocious battle in full pitch. As Fargo had feared, the poor marksmanship of the voyageurs had brought down only a few attackers. However, the hidden trip holes had thrown three riders violently to the ground, and all but one was picked off before they got to their feet.

No mercy, Fargo reminded himself, shooting the third outlaw as he tried to retreat. By Fargo's count that was ten men out of the fight, and Stone's ranks were considerably thinned.

Unfortunately, Bradford, hiding behind an oak, was having a field day. Even with the voyageurs in rifle pits, the trick shot rapidly scored three head shots.

Rip's Greener had one more load, and the gun roared now, Bradford's tree taking the brunt of the pellets. Crumbled bark flew into his eyes, rattling him, and the deadly shootist whirled to draw a bead on Rip.

Volcanic pistol barking in his left hand, Colt in his right, Fargo made it hot for Bradford, so much lead the outlaw danced like a marionette to avoid it. Rip retreated to cover.

The remaining outlaws were on the feather edge of panic. By now, dust and black-powder smoke hazed the battleground, and one rider carelessly charged too close to a position, impaling his horse on the pointed stakes. At this range, even the inexperienced boatmen were able to shoot the screaming man to confetti.

Two outlaws had swung wide and ridden up the riverbank, preparing to breach the defenses from behind. Fargo gigged the Ovaro forward and met the two with a double blast from the express gun. The powerful loads of buckshot shredded their upper bodies and ejected them from their saddles.

Sensing victory, and with the enemy ranks considerably thinned, Etienne shouted, *"Allons!"* and the voyageurs charged en masse. This snapped the back of the attack. The disorganized, thoroughly beaten enemy wheeled to retreat, but Fargo's powerful voice roared out:

"No mercy, boys! First the horses, then the men! Kill *all* of them!"

The Creoles followed orders, and not one man escaped. Two minutes later, the grisly task was complete. Fargo and Rip moved around the camp, finishing off the wounded and possum players.

"You notice two are missing?" Fargo said quietly to Rip.

"Ahuh. The two Winslowe brothers. The cowardly sons of bitches had it all planned out to hightail it if the battle went bad."

For the stalwart voyageurs, the outcome was much better. Three men killed, three slightly wounded.

"We goin' after Stone and Bradford?" Rip asked.

"Not just yet," Fargo said. "I'd like to run 'em down right now, but I gave my word to Medicine Flute. First we have a little rendezvous downriver."

Rip swore hotly. "We survive this shindig by sheer luck, and now we tempt fate agin? Like I said, Fargo—the pitcher can go once too often to the well."

18

The spot where Fargo told the Comanches to meet him was on the Indian side of Red River about halfway between Caswell Jones' camp and the location of that morning's battle. He and Rip pushed their mounts to a breakneck pace, for Fargo had promised to lend assistance in the initial stage of the attack.

They raced past gullies washed red with eroded soil and through hills dotted with bluebonnets and daisies. It was country, Fargo couldn't help thinking, too pretty for all this bloodletting. But the thugs and criminal profiteers, here in the lawless Indian Territory, were sprouting up like weeds on the landscape, and hard death was the only thing that could root them out—and discourage others in the future.

They rounded a sharp bend in the river, and Fargo hauled back on the reins.

"Up ahead is where I tied the rope last night," he told Rip. "Between that dogwood tree on the Texas side and that oak just ahead."

Rip cast a nervous glance around. "I don't see no Comanches."

"You never will until they *want* you to see them."

Fargo imitated a whip-poor-will, and at least a dozen renegades emerged from hiding, converging on them.

"You come just in time," Medicine Flute told Fargo. "Look there."

He followed the Comanche's finger and saw mirror flashes from a distant knoll—an Indian lookout.

"Boat be here soon," Medicine Flute said.

Rip had moved down to the water to examine the rope. "Fargo, you got it slantdicular," he called back. "Don't you want it straight across?"

"That's deliberate, old son. A straight rope stops a keelboat dead center in the river. That leaves the boatmen a clear line of fire straight toward each bank."

"I take your drift," Rip said. "This way she'll hang up crooked and throw off their line of fire."

"We hear battle upriver," Medicine Flute told Fargo. "You have killed the white dogs from the log post?"

"It's done," Fargo told him. "Dead to the last man. And like I told you last night, *this* battle is yours. I will help you only until the Comanches are clearly winning."

"I have ears for this. And you want nothing from the goods?"

Fargo shook his head. "All yours. Load 'em up on travois and haul 'em off."

A Comanche shouted something, and a moment later Caswell Jones' spoils vessel eased around a bend. Fargo and Rip hobbled their horses behind the brush.

Fargo pulled the Spencer from Rip's saddle scabbard. "Take this," he said, handing his Henry to his partner. "But I meant what I said, Rip. We've done enough killing today. Don't burn powder unless you have to—this ain't our picnic."

Rip nodded. "What I seen last night in their camp made me mad as a peeled rattler. It also proved this outfit needs to be dead as a can of corned beef. But I've supped full of killin' for one day."

The keelboat glided forward, square sail flat but with men poling along both sides. The Comanches, bows strung taut with arrows, dropped into the grass while Fargo and Rip slipped behind the big oak.

"Here she comes," Rip whispered, "and that no-account Caswell Jones is standin' right behind a one-pounder mounted on the rail. Mebbe they saw them Injin signals."

A one-pounder, Fargo fretted, that was likely filled with deadly canister shot. He knew the critical moment would come when the keelboat hit the rope—would it even hold? This was a big boat, and that rope had been underwater since last night.

If it did hold, Jones would order someone to cut it immediately, and Fargo's job was to prevent that long enough for the Comanches to gain the upper hand.

A slow, creaking groan told Fargo the rope had been hit—and was holding. "We've gut-hooked our fish," he told Rip, levering the Spencer.

Rip flashed his gap-toothed grin. "Look at him. That egg-suckin' varmint Jones don't know whether to shit or go blind."

The keelboat began to drift into a slant in midstream. Jones barked out an order, and a crewman with a knife leaped into the river. Before he could cut the rope, however, Fargo blew a huge chunk of the boat away only inches from the crewman's face. He gave up and swam to the safety of the opposite shore.

Fargo's shot triggered a spine-tingling war cry from the Comanches, who rose up firing a flurry of quartz-tipped arrows. Men fell, screaming, into the river. Jones leaped to the one-pounder, aimed it at the Comanches, and thumb-scratched a lucifer to life. Before he could lower it to the touchhole, however, Fargo's next shot punched through his chest and slammed the dead man back against the plank cabin, collapsing a wall.

Despite all the firearms aboard, seeing their captain killed took all the fight out of the crew. They leaped into the river and attempted to make it to the Texas shore.

"Big mistake," Fargo told Rip. "The easiest way to kill a man is when he's taking a crap or at least thigh-deep in water."

The fired-up Comanches knew this, too, and waded into the river in pursuit, killing with arrows, war hatchets, and knives. By now their steam was up and they gave no quarter. Some even swam to the opposite bank to scalp the wounded and dying, risking an unclean death if they drowned.

"Savage as a meat axe," Rip muttered, averting his eyes from the ghastly tableau. "Them sons of bitches deserve to die, Fargo, but I druther see 'em stretch hemp after a trial."

Fargo nodded. "Let's pull foot. We kept our word, and I can't stomach any more of this. Most tribes are rough warriors, but Comanches are pitiless."

As they retrieved their horses, Rip said, "Trailsman, you are a huckleberry above a persimmon, know that? This whole plan worked out just like you said it would."

Fargo hit leather. "I rolled the dice and got lucky, that's all. But I got one more account to settle, and it might be the hardest battle yet. So it's best to take the bull by the horns and get it over with."

Fargo and Rip rode hard to the west, stopping only to spell and cool out their horses. Fargo knew that Stone and Bradford had no intention of clearing out of the Indian Territory before they killed Belinda and the other prisoners—all witnesses against them.

"Hell, Fargo," Rip argued during their final break along the river, "they've had plenty of time to kill them and light out by now."

"They might have killed the prisoners," Fargo conceded. "But they'll be waiting for us, count on it. Especially me."

"What, on account of all the goods we cost 'em?"

"Those goods ain't worth an old underwear button compared to the two brothers I killed—to them, anyhow."

Rip nodded. "Ahuh, that shines. Besides, Bradford tried to brace you from the first time we seen him. It's been buildin' to a showdown twixt you two."

"That's the way of it. And now it's time to post the pony."

"Fargo, I've learned not to doubt you. But it'd be easier to tie down a bobcat with a piece of string than to outdraw that son of a bitch Bradford."

"Long as I send him over the mountains," Fargo said, stepping into leather, "and give him an even chance, it's a clean deal."

The two riders tethered their horses at the east end of the deserted mud-and-shanty hovel, then leapfrogged their way closer to the trading-post compound. Protected by the soddy where Fargo had killed Bo, the Trailsman shouted, "Bradford! It's me and you now, just like you wanted! I'm calling you out!"

Harsh laughter sounded within the log walls. "So the cowardly buckskin boy screwed up his courage? Well, Fargo, you ain't got the caliber for the job, but I'm more than happy to kill you."

The gate creaked open and Bradford stepped out, spurs jingling under a pair of thick bull-hide chaps.

Fargo handed Rip his Henry. "Keep an eye out for Stone. If he pokes his head out, ventilate it."

Fargo got a firm purchase on his resolve, then stepped into view. A good one hundred feet separated the men, and they slowly paced it off.

"I could kill you now, Fargo," Bradford boasted. "But I'll let you get closer, and I'll even let you go for your shooter first."

"I don't spit when you say hawk."

"Shit! You ain't got no choice, buckskin boy. You got any idea how many men I've bucked out in smoke?"

"No, but I watched you murder three innocent men today, and you'll soon be shoveling coal in hell for it."

"Oh, I'm quaking with fear. Don't you know only the unborn are innocent?" Bradford was closer, and Fargo heard his spurs clearly chinging. "*You?* You put me in hell? Don't blow smoke up my ass. I'll live to piss on your grave. You're just throwing a bluff."

Now, Fargo told himself. *Time to play your ace.*

Quicker than a striking snake, and well before Bradford expected, Fargo filled his hand with blue steel and got the drop on his enemy.

Bradford froze in midstep, his face going a few shades paler. "Hold on, Fargo. They say you go by the 'Code.' You know a draw-shoot can't commence until both men stop walking and go into their crouch. I wasn't ready."

"I know," Fargo said cheerfully. "So I won't shoot you. You'll get your even chance unless you make any quick moves, in which case I'll put daylight through you."

"All right, you had your chance to show off. I admit you're quicker than most. Now leather that shooter again and then *throw* it for real, you whoreson bastard!"

Fargo taunted him with a toothy grin. "You still ain't twigged the game, have you, mouth? *I'm* in charge here, and you're about to cash in for good."

"I double hog-tie *dare* you to face me on even terms, Fargo."

"I intend to—even, but on my terms."

"You only got the drop on me by cheating. Leather it, you cock-chafer. Then make your play! I won't live on the same earth with a shit-eating cur like you! Jerk it back, and I'll burn you where you stand!"

"All right, here's my play," Fargo said just before the Colt bucked in his hand.

Bradford leaped as if he'd been scalded, but the only thing Fargo hit was the hammer of his Remington, which had been blown completely off.

"The hell?" Bradford demanded, struck nearly speechless.

"You ain't worth a whorehouse token without a six-shooter, are you?" Fargo said, leathering his six-gun. "Just like a baby without his sugar tit."

Bradford's mouth twisted in rage. "You're a bald-faced liar, Fargo! You said we'd be shooting it out."

"No," Fargo corrected him. "As you yourself said, we'd be hugging. That just means a fight to the death, not a shootout."

"You mean . . . fists? I don't go in much for that."

"Takes too long to beat a man to death," Fargo said. "But I notice a bowie knife in your sheath—one with a ten-inch blade that can kill a bear. I'll put my Arkansas toothpick up against it."

Fargo raised his leg and jerked the toothpick from his boot.

"You *knew* I meant guns when I challenged you," Brad sputtered. "You can't just—"

"Shut pan," Fargo ordered, "you goddamn nickel-novel fool. I'll give it to you with the bark still on it, Winslowe: a man fights to his own strength, not his enemy's. You spent too much time trick-shooting, when you shoulda also been learning the blade— especially when you wear one for all to see. You'll die by the blade today, you murdering scut, and you'll die like a dog in the dirt."

Just then a gunshot rang out from inside the walled compound. Bradford laughed. "There goes your whore and her kin, Fargo. Guess you forgot about my brother. Stone ain't about to let you—"

"Skye!" Belinda's triumphant voice called out. "Skye, I just killed Stone Winslowe. We're all free now!"

It was Fargo's turn to laugh. "Well now, gunslinger—looks like you're the last Winslowe brother left. Briefly."

Bradford's eyes went smoky with rage. "I ain't in no funnin' mood, mister."

"Yessir," Fargo continued, starting to move in on his adversary, "too damn bad, ain't it? Sounds like Stone was took sick—all of a sudden like. You Winslowe boys been dropping fast—Clint, Bo, now Stone. 'Pears it's just you now, bowie boy. Let's get to huggin'."

Bradford licked his lips. "Say, Fargo, why not settle this some other way? Stone's got three thousand dollars tucked in his boot. That'll tide you for years."

"That money will go to Rebecca Halfpenny and the Starr family."

"Fargo, to hell with that sweet lavender crap, I can—"

"It's past peace-piping, blowhard." Fargo stopped only ten feet from his enemy. "Bridge the gap, trick shooter."

Bradford's hand started toward the knife in his sheath. Suddenly it plunged inside his shirt. But Fargo had figured him for a hideout gun, and already had his right arm cocked. Bradford had the over-and-under derringer halfway out of his shirt when the Arkansas toothpick sliced into his heart, ripping it open.

Winslowe's high-pitched scream of pain rent the air. The twitching body stood for a few seconds while spuming blood hit the ground with an obscene slapping sound. Then Bradford crumpled in an awkward heap.

Rarely, a body showed nervous reflex even with a ruined heart. The legs kept jerking, and despite his contempt for this murderer, Fargo lacked the stomach to leave him twitching in the dirt. He stilled him with a finishing shot.

Rip walked up beside him. "All holler and no heart—in a manner of speakin'. But I see you take no pleasure in killin' him."

Fargo shook his head. "No pleasure—and no regrets."

"Ahuh. Like you told them frogs—no mercy."

"Not in a place," Fargo said, "where law can't come in. It's summary justice, old campaigner, and that's all we got—*just us*."

19

Fargo and Rip lifted a trap in the raw lumber floor and climbed down a few wooden rungs into the dank underground chamber beneath the trading post. Belinda held a coal-oil lamp so they could see the windowless chamber where her family and Rebecca Halfpenny had been held prisoners for months.

"I don't think I could've survived it," Fargo finally said. "Cooped up like a caged animal. No sky, no sun, no stars. I suspected something like this, but I didn't want to press Belinda."

"Damn near no food, neither," Rip tossed in.

"This is what you two brave men saved us from, Mr. Fargo," Louise Starr, Belinda's mother, said through the trapdoor in the floor.

"It was just horrible, Skye," Belinda said. "The entrance is right behind the counter, but Stone kept it locked except when I was allowed to take food down once a day."

Stone lay in a crumpled heap on the floor near Fargo's feet.

"He locked me in with the rest when he rode out this morning," Belinda said. "But I had a gun in my dress. When he came back, he climbed down here and drew a gun, so I killed him. And I'm *glad* I did."

The three climbed back up into the trading post, where the rest stood waiting, pale, emaciated faces aglow with the joy of being freed. Fargo screwed up his courage and gazed into Rebecca's eyes.

"Mrs. Halfpenny, about Justin, I—"

"Shush, you wonderful man, just shush. I know all about Justin, and it was *not* your fault. You and Mr. Miller performed a Herculean task in getting us free."

"Not to mention," put in Joshua Starr, "the lives they have saved by breaking up this river pirate operation."

"Gee whillikens, Mr. Fargo," little Scotty piped up. "You really *do* wear buckskins. Don't they scratch like the dickens?"

Fargo and the rest laughed. "Sometimes they itch a mite, Scotty, but I've never had to sew up a tear. Maybe you can talk your ma into making you some."

"Consider it done," Louise promised. "He'll be the little Trailsman."

Fargo grinned. "That's a fine compliment, ma'am."

He glanced around the nearly empty trading post. "Folks, Etienne will be anchoring here sometime tomorrow. Are any of your possessions left?"

"See that partition dividing this room?" Joshua replied. "That wood used to be our two wagons. The canvas they used to make their thirst parlors. As for our furniture, Belinda says they busted it up to make bonfires when you two gents had them scared spitless."

"It's just as well," Fargo said. "You wouldn't be safe traveling alone through this territory. I talked to Etienne, and he'll make room for all of you on the keelboat. That will get you to Wichita Falls. You folks found enough money on Stone to hold you for quite a while."

"What about this place, Skye?" Belinda asked. "Are you just going to leave it?"

"Not hardly, lady. It'll just tempt the next pack of wild curs." He pointed to a wooden keg on a side shelf. "There's enough black powder there to blow this place sky-high, and once you're all safely on the boat, that's exactly what I aim to do."

"It's all so ironic," Belinda said. "All four of the Winslowe brothers dead, and for what? Stupid greed that got them nowhere. Ma, it reminds me of that nursery rhyme you used to tell me:

> The King of France,
> He had ten thousand men,
> He marched them up a hill one day,
> And marched them down again."

"Honey," Rip said, "you're pretty as four aces, but that's too far north for me. Let's all rustle up some grub and *eat*."

Billowing black clouds rose high into a pure blue sky the color of a gas flame. The phony trading post that spelled misery for so many was now merely a bad memory.

The keelboat lay at anchor about two hundred feet upstream of the former outlaw hellhole. Fargo, preparing to scout ahead, secured his bedroll and slicker under the cantle straps.

"Rip," he called to the old codger, "how'd you like a job slinging hash for the boat crew? One of the men killed yesterday was the cook, and Etienne would like to hire you on."

"Square deal?" Rip hurried down the gangplank. "Back to slinging hash, huh? Well, make a plow horse but spoil a racer."

Fargo snorted. "You old clodpole, you're twenty years past your racing days."

"Ahuh, but I just got done sidin' the Trailsman while he cleaned up the Indian Territory."

"And a fair-to-middling partner, too, for a jasper that can remember the days of knee breeches and powdered wigs."

Rip scowled. "Does your mother know you're out, sonny? Anyhow, hell yes, I'll take the job. These frogs is pretty good lads after all, but they'll get none a them crawdads nor blue crabs from Rip Miller—I cook American. Hash and stew and corn dodgers. Say . . . speakin' of cleaning up the Indian Territory—"

"Don't worry," Fargo cut him off. "I didn't forget about the reward Niles offered. I'll ride north today."

"He'll take your word for it?"

"Of course he would," Fargo said, "but he won't have to. You forget about the moccasin telegraph. He'll know it all before I get there."

Fargo noticed Belinda strolling his way, a mysterious smile on her face as she pulled a horn comb through her golden tresses. She wore a calico skirt and a crisp white shirtwaist. If Fargo didn't know better, he'd have sworn she was wearing a corset, but it would be wasted on her.

"Say," he told Rip, almost forgetting what they'd been talking about, "why'n't you scare up some grub?"

Rip saw the comely lass approaching and lowered his voice.

"Won't be long, you two'll be doin' the mazy waltz agin, you lucky son of a bitch."

Rip went aboard the boat again.

"Riding out?" Belinda said, her tone disappointed.

"That's what I'm paid to do."

"So I won't . . . see you again?" she pouted.

"Oh, you'll be seeing me just about every night," Fargo assured her.

"Wonderful! Maybe we can go out . . . picking berries."

"I like berries," Fargo assured her.

"Good!" Rip's voice interrupted from the nearby plank cabin, where he was obviously eavesdropping. "Soon's you two bring me them berries, I'll make you a cobbler."

LOOKING FORWARD!
The following is the opening
section of the next novel in the exciting
***Trailsman* series from Signet:**

THE TRAILSMAN #340
HANNIBAL RISING

Deep in the Missouri backwoods, 1861—
where hate and greed pit brother against brother
and sister against sister.

There were only two things in life Skye Fargo liked as much
as a good card game. One was a willing filly and the other was
the warm feeling in his gut from good whiskey. At the moment
he was enjoying all three. As the locals in Missouri might say,
he was in hog heaven.

Fargo was on the steamboat *Yancy*, a side-wheeler plying its
way up the broad Mississippi River toward the small town of
Hannibal. He had sat in on a poker game early that afternoon
and now it was ten at night and he was on a winning streak that
he hoped would continue a good long while. Perched on his lap
was a dove called Sweetpea and at his elbow sat a half-empty
bottle of the best whiskey the *Yancy* served.

Fargo took another swallow, smacked his lips in satisfaction, and then lightly smacked Sweetpea on her rounded back-

side. "Stick with me, gal, and this will be a night you won't forget."

"Where have I heard that before?" Sweetpea giggled and fluttered her long eyelashes. She had a full bosom and a slim waist and lips as red and full as ripe strawberries. Her hair was a lustrous burgundy and hung to her shoulders in curls.

Fargo smacked her again, harder. That giggle of hers irritated him. It had a nasal quality, as if she was giggling out her nose instead of her mouth, and made him think of a goose being strangled. She did it a lot. Her voluptuous body more than made up for the annoyance but if she giggled less he would be happier. And it wasn't as if she was the only irritation. The other was a man named Baxter, a weasel with a needle-thin mustache and a derby who fancied himself a professional gambler and had been needling the other players the whole day. Fargo was growing tired of being needled.

"Are you going to bet or sit there fondling that cow?" Baxter now demanded.

Sweetpea stiffened. "Here now. There's no call for insults."

"Tell that to that slab of muscle you've attached yourself to," the gambler replied. "If everyone put on the same show he does when he goes to bet, poker games would last weeks."

The three others players shifted uneasily in their chairs. They had grown tired of his carping, too.

Fargo sat perfectly still. He was a big man, broad of shoulder, and he did pack more hard muscle on his frame than most. It came from the life he led. His buckskins marked him for what he was: a frontiersman. He also wore a white hat nearly brown with dust, a red bandanna around his throat, and boots that had seen a lot of wear. On his hip was a Colt, in a hidden sheath in his boot an Arkansas toothpick. He kept his beard neatly trimmed and had what a lady once described as "the most piercing lake blue eyes this side of creation." Now he raised those eyes to meet the gambler's and the lake blue became glacier cold. "For such a little runt you sure do run off at the mouth."

Now it was Baxter who stiffened. He wore a frock coat that might conceal all sorts of things and during the game had held his left forearm on the table in a way that suggested to Fargo he had something up his sleeve. A hideout, most likely. "I don't like that kind of talk."

"Then you shouldn't go around insulting folks." Fargo added chips to the pots. "I raise you, you little peckerwood."

Baxter grew red in the face. He was short, not much over five feet, and about as wide as a broom handle. "Keep it up."

Fargo gripped Sweetpea by the arm and pulled her off his lap. She frowned but didn't object. Standing, he lowered his hand so it brushed his Colt. "I am tired of your guff. Shut up or show you have sand."

The other players pushed back their chairs.

Baxter glowered. He glanced at Fargo's Colt and shifted slightly so his left arm was pointed at Fargo. "You don't want to rile me."

"I'm plumb scared."

"I mean it. Ask anyone here. I have a reputation."

"Makes two of us."

"Is that so? Just who the hell are you, anyway? I've said my name but I don't recollect you ever saying yours."

"It's Skye Fargo."

The gambler blinked and started to smirk as if he thought it was a jest and then he gave a start and the red in his cheeks drained to a pasty chalk. "I think I've heard of you."

"Could be," Fargo allowed. The damn newspapers were always writing about him.

Another player said, "I sure have. You're the one who killed those outlaws a while back. The ones that robbed that stage. I read where you went up against twenty of them armed with just your bowie and your pistols."

Fargo didn't own a bowie. He wore one revolver, not two. And there had been four cutthroats, not twenty.

Baxter looked sick. He had broke out in a sweat and his fingers were twitching. "You're *that* Fargo?"

Fargo didn't answer.

The other players were staring at the gambler as if they would a man about to step up on a gallows. Baxter's throat bobbed and he coughed and said, "I didn't know who you were when I said all those things."

Fargo waited, his hand close to his Colt.

"I saw you look at my sleeve. I suppose you've guessed I have a derringer up it."

Fargo waited.

"If I try to use it you're liable to kill me."

"You'll be dead before it clears your sleeve," Fargo broke his silence.

Baxter started to raise his other arm to his face as if to mop it with his sleeve but thought better of it. "Listen. How about if I say I'm sorry and we get on with the game? No hard feelings?"

"Say it." Fargo had no real hankering to resort to gunplay. But he would be damned if he would take any more insults.

"What? Oh. All right. I apologize. Will that do?"

Fargo slowly sank into his chair. They all heard the breath Baxter let out.

The other players slid their chairs to the table and Sweetpea pressed against Fargo's leg and wriggled to show she would like to reclaim his lap. He let her but he shifted slightly so he had quick access to his Colt.

Baxter cleared his throat again. "I never met anyone famous before. Not unless you count a senator."

Fargo refilled his glass and took another swallow. The whiskey tasted flat, and he frowned.

"Mind if I ask what you're doing in this neck of the woods? Folks say you're partial to the prairie country and the mountains."

Fargo's frowned deepened. The gambler had gone from being one kind of nuisance to being another. "I am partial to not being pestered."

"Oh. Sorry."

Baxter fell into a sulk. The other players were uneasy and it showed. For Fargo, the joy had gone out of the whiskey and now the game, and he was mad at himself for spoiling things. The next hand, he bet half his winnings on three kings and was beat by a full house. He could take a hint. He announced he was calling it quits for the night.

Sweetpea stayed glued to his side as he cashed in his chips and watched him put the money in his poke and tuck the poke under his shirt. Beaming, she hooked her arm in his. "Does this mean we can go for a stroll? I would dearly love some fresh air."

So would Fargo. The cigar and pipe smoke was thick enough to cut with a butter knife.

The hurricane deck was almost empty at that time of night. Over in a corner a couple were cheek to cheek. Another man and woman at the port rail were gazing at the myriad of stars that sparkled in the firmament.

Fargo strolled past them to the jackstaff. Thick coils of smoke belched from the smokestack aft of the deck and were borne away on the breeze. The throb of the steam engine never let up. He gazed down at the murky water and listened to the hiss of the bow as it cleaved the surface.

"I lost a good friend last week on the *Celeste Holmes*," Sweetpea sadly remarked.

Fargo had heard about the disaster. A boiler blew and over sixty people were scalded to death. The *Celeste* limped on, only to run into a snag that ripped her open from bow to stern. According to the few survivors, the boat broke apart down the middle and a second explosion blew most of what was left, and nearly everyone still alive, to bits and pieces.

"They say that pretty near ten boats have gone down in the past couple of years."

Fargo grunted.

Sweetpea bit her lip and twirled a curl with her finger. "I have nightmares about it happening to me."

"If it scares you, why work on one?"

She shrugged. "Jobs are hard to come by. This one is easy and it pays well and I don't have to sleep with a man unless I want to."

Pulling her to him, Fargo cupped her fanny and grinned. "If you want to sleep with me I won't fight you off."

Giggling, Sweetpea pecked him on the chin. "I like you, handsome. You're fun to be with and you treat a girl decent."

"Only until I get her in bed." Fargo nuzzled her neck and was rewarded with a coo of delight.

"Why can't all men be as playful as you? Most only want to get the poke over with and be shed of the woman. Why is that?"

Fargo nipped an earlobe and was running the tip of his tongue from her ear to her mouth when the *pat-pat-pat* of rushing feet on the hardwood deck registered. He reacted in instinct, and whirled.

There were two of them, a man and a woman. Steel glittered, and the man came at him with a knife.

Pushing Sweetpea out of harm's way, Fargo dodged a cut that would have gutted him like a fish. He couldn't see their faces all that well but he was sure he had never run into either of them before, which made their attempt to kill him all the more bewildering. Shaking off his surprise, he swooped his hand to his Colt but before he could clear leather the woman sprang with lightning speed and gripped his arm.

"I have him! Do it!"

The man's teeth flashed white and he thrust his blade up and in.

Fargo's boot was already rising. He caught the would-be assassin between the legs and the knife stopped inches from his chest as the man gasped and staggered back, his thighs pinched together from the pain.

Suddenly the woman holding him let go and a knife glinted in her hand.

"I will kill you myself."

She had a slight accent that at the moment Fargo couldn't afford to give much thought to. He barely avoided a stab at his throat. Pivoting, he went for his Colt again, only to have the woman do the most incredible thing; she leaped high into the air and kicked him with her right foot, catching him across the jaw. Pain exploded as he skipped back out of reach.

Fargo collided with someone behind him. A squawk from Sweetpea told him who. Their legs became entangled and down they went. Dreading the sharp slice of steel into his ribs, Fargo shoved clear and rose to his knees. This time he got the Colt out—but there was no one to shoot.

The pair were fleeing across the hurricane deck, the woman helping the man, his arm over her shoulder.

Another couple, the two who were admiring the stars, had come running over and were agape with astonishment.

Fargo gave chase. He lost sight of his quarry in the inky shadow of the overhang. He had his choice of right or left and went to the right to the head of a passageway that ran nearly the entire length of the steamboat. Enough light filtered from the cabins and from the few lamps to reveal there wasn't anyone within fifty feet. Quickly, he turned and flew to the head of the other passageway but the only person close enough was an elderly matron hobbling on a cane.

Fargo had lost them. He ran toward the matron, who drew back as if afraid he was going to attack her. "Did you see two people run past? A man and a woman?"

"The only person I've seen in a hurry is you."

Fargo sprinted on but there was no sign of them. He couldn't understand it. They hadn't had time to get very far. He wondered if they had ducked into one of the forward cabins and retraced his steps, the matron shying away from him as if he were loco.

Around the corner came Sweetpea and the stargazers. Squealing with relief, Sweetpea threw herself at him and hugged him close.

"Skye! Thank goodness you're all right! Who were they? Why were they trying to kill you?"

"I wish to hell I knew."

The other couple, middle-aged and portly, were holding hands. "We couldn't believe our eyes, Maude and me," the man said.

The woman nodded. "Harold and I saw them run at you and that young man draw his knife."

"You got a good look at them?"

"Only a glimpse. They were over in the corner. We thought they were lovers."

Fargo remembered the couple standing cheek to cheek in the shadows. "Why did you say the man was young?" He hadn't been able to tell much, as dark as it was.

"Just an impression I had," Maude answered.

"Were they on the deck before you got there?"

"Now that I think about it," Harold said, "no, they weren't. They showed up just a bit before you did."

Fargo rubbed his sore jaw and pondered. It made no damn sense.

"Maybe they saw you win big at the poker table and were out to help themselves to your poke," Sweetpea said.

"Could be." Fargo had a hunch there was more to it. The pair had been as fiercely intent as starved wolves out to bring down a bull elk.

"Let's hope they don't try again."

"Oh my," Maude declared. "Wouldn't that be positively awful?"

No other series packs this much heat!

THE TRAILSMAN

#320: OREGON OUTRAGE
#321: FLATHEAD FURY
#322: APACHE AMBUSH
#323: WYOMING DEATHTRAP
#324: CALIFORNIA CRACKDOWN
#325: SEMINOLE SHOWDOWN
#326: SILVER MOUNTAIN SLAUGHTER
#327: IDAHO GOLD FEVER
#328: TEXAS TRIGGERS
#329: BAYOU TRACKDOWN
#330: TUCSON TYRANT
#331: NORTHWOODS NIGHTMARE
#332: BEARTOOTH INCIDENT
#333: BLACK HILLS BADMAN
#334: COLORADO CLASH
#335: RIVERBOAT RAMPAGE
#336: UTAH OUTLAWS
#337: SILVER SHOWDOWN
#338: TEXAS TRACKDOWN

**Follow the trail of the gun-slinging heroes of
Penguin's Action Westerns at
penguin.com/actionwesterns**

"A writer in the tradition of Louis L'Amour
and Zane Grey!"
—*Huntsville Times*

National Bestselling Author
RALPH COMPTON

AUTUMN OF THE GUN
THE KILLING SEASON
THE DAWN OF FURY
BULLET CREEK
RIO LARGO
DEADWOOD GULCH
A WOLF IN THE FOLD
TRAIL TO COTTONWOOD FALLS
BLUFF CITY
THE BLOODY TRAIL
SHADOW OF THE GUN
DEATH OF A BAD MAN
RIDE THE HARD TRAIL
BLOOD ON THE GALLOWS
BULLET FOR A BAD MAN
THE CONVICT TRAIL
RAWHIDE FLAT
OUTLAW'S RECKONING
THE BORDER EMPIRE
THE MAN FROM NOWHERE
SIXGUNS AND DOUBLE EAGLES
BOUNTY HUNTER
FATAL JUSTICE

**Available wherever books are sold or at
penguin.com**